Also by Jo Hamya

Three Rooms

The Hypocrite

The Hypocrite

Jo Hamya

WEIDENFELD & NICOLSON

First published in Great Britain in 2024 by Weidenfeld & Nicolson
an imprint of The Orion Publishing Group Ltd
Carmelite House, 50 Victoria Embankment
London EC4Y 0DZ

An Hachette UK Company

1 3 5 7 9 10 8 6 4 2

Epigraph on p.v: 'Lions on Leashes' from COVENTRY by Rachel Cusk.
Copyright © Rachel Cusk, 2019, used by permission of The Wylie Agency
(UK) Limited.

A CIP catalogue record for this book is
available from the British Library.

ISBN (Hardback) 978 1 3996 1322 4
ISBN (Export Trade Paperback) 978 1 3996 1323 1
ISBN (eBook) 978 1 3996 1325 5
ISBN (Audio) 978 1 3996 1326 2

Typeset by Input Data Services Ltd, Bridgwater, Somerset

Printed in Great Britain by Clays Ltd, Elcograf S.p.a.

www.weidenfeldandnicolson.co.uk
www.orionbooks.co.uk

I. *'To be an artist is to have your creation obey you, but . . . parenthood is the opposite of art: the created object – the child – can become instead an uncontrollable source of destructiveness . . .'*

II. *'I find that I do not believe in the child-killing as a literal event . . . Ours is a world in which psychological and actual violence have become mutually distinct. The killing no longer means what it might have. Actual violence is rudimentary and mute; psychological violence is complex and articulate.'*

Rachel Cusk, 'Lions on Leashes', from *Coventry* (2019)

PREVIEW:
DECISION TO LEAVE

There was summer, a beach; a country they were still getting used to in the early stages of their holiday. There was a map of tourists on the sand with bared stomachs on striped towels, rows of skin pillowed up to brown in the sun. There was – ahead – the shoreline, the plastic rainbow litter of miniaturised buckets and trowels. Other people's husbands standing desultorily over their spawn while their wives took a break, took Aperol, wore designer sunglasses, half watched little sand huts being drawn up: the erection of child-sized city-states on the coast, subject to parental patience and barely developed motor skills. There were teenaged girls in their first bikinis flirting with the local boys, and officiate beach wardens in navy polo shirts and navy shorts, lips half pursed around their whistles: eyes flickering to them, then away.

August. Sicilian islands. Sophia had taken her father out to sea. It happened naturally. She tugged his hand. She was, at that point, so much smaller than him. Her cheeks were as soft as the just-forming paunch of his stomach. The sides of her mouth were bearded with pulverised peach flesh, and clinging beach grit. Her fingers were unpleasantly

3

sticky. She did not look like a serious person. But when she said, *we go now*, he hadn't been able to imagine staying still. He took her hand and made himself move. It was hard. There was—

her little hand tugging—

(and the task of stooping to reach it; the cramped space left to pick up his knees in, and the soreness around his back, which had been a terrible new sensation in those days—)

her little hand tugging—

(the weather, which had been too warm: he hated beach-wear, he had worn linen trousers in protest, he thought they looked quite good—)

her hand pulling faster—

(and the sudden fear: that they had not brought toys – one of those crude red moulds of seashells she could have slapped onto the sand or an inflatable ball, though he wasn't sure how well throwing and catching would go; the thing would have probably floated out on the water if she tried, so the question of how to entertain her, how to have fun, turned helplessly in his mind—)

they reached the shore.

Sophia's mother watched them from the shade of a rented umbrella. Once they reached the sea, Sophia sat down in the water. Her father scooped her immediately back up. Patches of pink dress near her legs and her bottom turned mauve instead: came up wetly, like a bruise. It seemed to bother him more than her. On being set down, she'd shrugged; moved two paces forward, sat down again. She'd begun pulling fistfuls of sand up and lumping them into a mound. After some consideration, her father crouched down too – rolled up the sleeves of his button-up and his trousers.

He'd started gathering sand into his palms, sculpting more carefully than his daughter. He'd added a moat. He'd taken pebbles and stuck them near the tower's base; made his hand into a claw and dripped slurries of sodden material over the edifice until the sand formed turrets. Each time his daughter made to help, he batted her fingers away. Sophia's mother watched her do battle over a sandcastle; watched her pout and knock parts off as they were added. Her father laughing. Continuing to build.

It had been exhausting to guard. Sophia's mother knew the beginnings of a tantrum when she saw one. Earlier that day she had used one arm to lift her daughter slightly above ground and another to slip a pair of blue gingham shorts under her feet while she thrashed. She'd tied a ribbon in the middle of the fabric's elasticated waist, she'd smoothed cotton. When it was done, Sophia had scowled. She shook her head. She prepared her bottom lip for conflict.

This was a daily ritual. Sophia knew what she wanted. Another change of clothes. Another. Her father worked on his novel in the other room.

The beach; the fat pulse of the sun and its resultant waves of lightheadedness. Sophia's mother touched her watch. She imagined swimming. She thought about how to do dinner that night, remembered dinner the night before – courtesy of her husband's friend. Someone he hadn't seen in years, another writer, whose daughter had been paid €15 to look after Sophia. A table of eight other strangers her husband was excited to meet again. She sat on the far side of the arrangement, away from him. That she could not keep track of their names, though evidently few people knew hers. That she had worried whether a sixteen-year-old she didn't know was equipped enough to take care of her child. That it had been a night of *not* speaking, with a glass of red wine hovering under her chin by its stem, and recollections pooled by the others from university pubs she'd never been near. And – *Aren't you stunning?* her least favourite of them said; gestured to the man she had married six years ago. *Has he shagged you yet?*

A pause. A smile. An argument on the way home.

By the sea, Sophia's protests had subsided into laughter instead: she'd learned to make a sport of demolishment. Her mother wondered whether she had enough good humour to deliver her daughter's hat before she got sunburn, whether she'd put enough SPF on; considered the thick square of black polyester-elastane blend flattening her breasts and mulled over whether she had the time to buy something nicer. She was tired.

When she woke from her nap, the time on the umbrella had run out. It, her husband, and child were gone. There'd been no note to explain the latter's departure, but she could picture it. Him, gathering Sophia up, awkward but sure, with one hand supporting her thighs and the other on her shoulder. Her mouth level with his ear. He liked to steal her away like that from time to time. When he did it, he would say something inane like, *Mummy needs a break*, and smile at his own benevolence. It's an image she resented: a middle-aged man in damp linen trousers, carrying her daughter. When a beach warden had asked whether, for the discounted price of €2.50, she would like the umbrella back, it had been the kindest thing she had ever heard.

PRE-SHOW:
A WOMAN OVER A TANNOY
IS ASKING AUDIENCE MEMBERS
TO TAKE THEIR SEATS

August, 2020. The back of the theatre is located on the west side of the building. Your first point of contact is Goods In. It looks like an industrial garage – yellow walls, yellow floor. Wire racks stacked with stickered cardboard boxes attend them. Fresh air filters through the gap between the ground and the immense roll-up door, and the men who keep it all running move in perfectly ordained paths while they speak into headsets; while they coordinate deliveries for the gift shop and the costume department; receive post for the entire building; handle packages marked CAUTION: HEAVY, and CAUTION: FRAGILE.

You keep moving. More slender lines of corridor. Front of house, ticket admin, and a bar take up only a tenth of the theatre: they form its visitor entrance. Back here, things flicker at you as you pass. Electricians are measuring out lengths of wire. A woman is sewing individual strands of hair into a lace cap. Another is washing a set of brushes, each with differently shaped heads: fanned and thin, fat and triangular; she is screwing caps onto pots of powder and rouge. A man in black jeans hurries past you, caressing a headset with a mouth that needs *a venti fucking oat latte with two pumps of vanilla syrup and a small, cold bottle of sparkling water, and please, watch them make that fucking coffee this time, do you hear me?*

Out of another doorway the scene looks positively corporate. In a room full of cubicles, fake ficus plants on tiny desks are getting watered by garbage language conversations about theatre memberships and arts funding: evergreen to the tune of *sustain the arts to sustain the future* spoken by tired employees' wilting mouths.

You pass the dressing rooms and studios. This side of the building gets no natural light. The bins are full of discarded Tesco meal deals – lettuce flattened with bad mayonnaise clings onto plastic sacks. You angle your body out of the way when racks of lighting or clothing are pushed past you with blunt, customary efficiency, until finally, you make it to a lift

—and step in.

When the doors open, the space revealed is black. Lights are rigged above your head, waiting to be used. Cables run the perimeter of the floor. The wall furthest from you is criss-crossed with wood; lit by glowing plastic boxes. It's disconcerting, but on stepping out of the wings, your eyes adjust and red seeps in. There, the expected rows of velvet chairs. The balconies overhead, trimmed with bands of gold metal, and the ceiling gessoed with angels.

It takes a moment to realise that the area you are standing in is, itself, not red – does not look like it belongs to the rest of the space at all. There is no wire racking. Instead, the back wall you thought was framed with wood has windows on this side, and something like daylight streaming out of them, too. Underneath, a counter. Saucepans and a knife block.

Behind you, backstage. Now, a kitchen. You move to its centre.

It has been dressed so beautifully, so convincingly, that it is hard not to go to the fridge and check for milk, and eggs and cheese. It is hard to believe that there are people holding walkie-talkies and phones on the floors below. You can't be sure but it's possible that even the smell of things is different here: like dill, and oranges. You lift the sugar bowl from its place on the kitchen table. There is sugar inside.

In his North London kitchen, Sophia's father measures out two teaspoons of sugar and stirs them into his cup. There is a leftover plate in front of him smeared with apple preserves and dough. He takes it to the sink. On the counter, the *Evening Standard* urges him to take advantage of the country's new-found freedom by tucking into oysters at Vinegar Yard, by seeing Titian conquer love and death at the National Gallery; it asks him to *eat out to help out*, a phrase even he has grown bored of turning into a joke by way of past lovers' genitalia. The paper extols the benefits of a UK-based 'staycation' – a word he has crossed out by hand in vermilion pen.

One evening in April, after a month of making small-talk in his local corner shop with whoever could bear to stand near him for an hour, he sat in front of a pixelated image of the foreign secretary, whose hands conducted such nightly proceedings in absence of the prime minister – he had fallen ill. A gold wedding band had flashed forward with statesmanlike authority while Sophia's father heard *change to our social-distancing measures now would risk a significant increase in the spread*; while he heard *damage to the economy over a longer period*; while he heard *measures must remain in place for at least the next three weeks.* The hazmat-inspired podium on-screen played on with other speakers for the duration of an hour. He'd called Sophia first. When she didn't pick up, he called her mother instead and howled. It's not something his daughter knows about. She'd sent him a text the following morning with a smiley face, having only just recharged her phone. His ex-wife was already in the guest bedroom, unpacking a suitcase into its wardrobe when he cried in slower, longer breaths the second time, and lingered over the typed-out emoticon. With great patience, she taught him how to install a popular new form of video-call software as a way to breach this new form of distance.

Not seeing Sophia, in itself, was not an uncommon event. When his ex-wife left him, there were no arguments about who their daughter would go with. She had been small enough to need constant care he felt it was more natural for her mother to give, and which he couldn't, because of his work. Gaps in contact became part of their relationship. He took care to mend them – with humour, with presents, and affection. He always wanted to know what she was turning into while she was gone.

During the months in which it had been unclear whether it was safe to see Sophia in person or not, his ex-wife had tactfully left the house once a week under the guise of shopping for food while his daughter moved haltingly across his screen, voice cutting and returning out of sync, face bleached by light coming in from a window in her background. When the calls finished, his ex-wife would reappear with stems of tulips he'd never have thought to buy for himself when alone. He'd watched her move about the house in clothes she'd worn when they were married.

She left him again yesterday. Today, he sets his coffee down on the fat lip of the bathroom's sink and rakes a comb through his hair. He clips his nails and rubs cream into his hands, takes a clothes brush over the light wool of his grey suit. Twenty minutes later, a cab dispenses him in front of a theatre in Covent Garden.

Quarter to two in the afternoon. The first thing he does is text Sophia to say he has made it. He sends a smiley face as an afterthought. Then, he lights a cigarette by the building's edge and searches the crossing to his right. Traffic. Horns coming up from the Strand. People's sandals, jackets, bags, scurrying past. There's a woman with her head bent and her thumb on her phone – such an ugly position, he finds. But she has a beautiful olive face and he likes the red colour of her shoes, so he counts her in the composition. She has stopped on the pavement. Now, he is outlining her: making more manifest the jewel drop earrings among her hair and the bangles on her wrist. There's her calf, her thigh. There's the twist of summer dress on her chest. As though she knows it would please him, she puts her phone in her pocket and tips her head back at the sky. He has the sun on her face. Who else could make her beautiful like this?

He does it for everyone: today is a benevolent day. A waiter in the restaurant to his left drops a tray he is using to lay silverware on the tables outside, and it's not *unpercussive*, the noise it makes – he can add it, somehow, to the thrum, to the music he imagines in his head. It might be excessive, but he makes the silk anemones on the restaurant's windows shake in their pots when it happens, little purple-pink shivers in green. The inside of the theatre ahead is visible through glass walls: the people within are like marionettes, waiting to be moved. When the cigarette goes out, he puts on a cotton mask and goes in.

Now, the presence of others. He waits in a queue elongated by the space individuals keep between themselves and others. Collects his ticket, stub of stiff white; is given an orange plastic square in exchange for his suit jacket. It's a trade down rather than off, but the room is hot. He is approached, gingerly, on whether he would like to buy a programme for £10 and accepts. Then he is served bad-wedding kind of wine at the bar, cold-misted glass smeared by hot fingers and not enough poured in: he regrets asking for it. It costs £10.25. Still, he enjoys himself. It's the contained way everything exists in a theatre. Everyone around him is doing the same: ticket, bag check, programme, drinks. Everyone is sipping the same sweating, overpriced alcohol and comparing notes on their pamphlets. If he came here tomorrow, he would find everything identical. It's a relief that things are normal, with only slight alterations. The half-faces, with eyes peering over cloth. The arrows on the floor, directing movement. They go mostly ignored.

The thing about the theatre foyer is that it has been recently renovated. The open-plan glass extension that spills seamlessly into the old front of house is new: there was less space before. The wall that has been taken down used to display posters of past and ongoing performances. There had been a greater sense of being ushered into the depths of the building, of exiting the world for a few hours to see something less real than what was outside. There had been no windows. The embrace of artificial light. How it is now, transparent, and stippled with other buildings' shadows, with London streaming in full view, is, he supposes, a new sensibility being asked of the arts. But even so, there are good things about the building's new set-up. At almost two o'clock, in the height of summer, the sun comes in. The foyer, where it meets the theatre's front of house, turns everything into a glasshouse where he can watch things grow.

Three-quarters of Sophia's audience is made up of young people in their twenties and early thirties. They cluster in groups, leaving around them empty space. They know each other's presence is the potential for sickness or death, and so they display an exquisitely exaggerated consideration in keeping to themselves. They take pictures of everything. The gold balustrades on stairways, the carved walls. They take pictures of themselves. Everything about them is as immaculate as a painting: colour, pose, poise. Their fingers and dexterous wrists, managing their camera phones. None of them lean back, or let their mouths unconsciously drop open. They take off their masks and become plastic, perfectly suspended with arched backs and pursed lips. He sees them pretend to do things like drink wine or read their programme before tucking away their devices to drink wine and read their programmes. He enjoys watching them, and so it is almost a shame when a woman wearing a headset touches his elbow. But he likes the way she tunes her eyes fluidly into a smile above her mask. He has attempted this before and failed. She does it well. She does it so it looks real; instructs him by her example to match the same quick change of pace. She's head of brand engagement and social media for the theatre, she says. She is working on his daughter's play. They have half an hour until it starts. Would he like a quick tour?

She leads him to a wood-panelled lift. Its doors open instantly for her. She points at his drink, apologises and says, you'll have to leave this; turns her head like a saint while he unhooks the cotton around his mouth and drains his medium measure of white in two awkward slugs. He leaves the glass next to a bouquet of lilies on the table beside them.

Plum carpets and mirrors on the surrounding walls. He must be very proud of Sophia following after him, the woman tells him while the lift takes them up. If she had a famous author for a father, she's not sure she would do the same.

Yes, of course, he says, he is very proud, though he doesn't know how accurate the word 'famous' is. She assumes he's being modest; tells him she had to google his name for a picture reference of who to find in the foyer. The results had turned up his *Desert Island Discs*, a *Telegraph* article ranking him one of a hundred most important people in twentieth-century British culture, a well-stocked Wikipedia page.

Sophia's father demurs. For all this so-called fame, she

still had to google what he looked like, who he was.

It was meant as a joke, but he can see he's embarrassed her. He starts to say, and Sophia's play? Do you like it? – only for the lift doors to open. She looks at him expectantly, says, Please, and waits for him to step out. Two awkward steps. He's sorry, he pleads with her. He doesn't know where to go.

Now she smiles in that same skilful way, with all of the uncovered parts of her face, as though something has been restored. It's just this way, she allows, and leads him forward. He watches the back of her head recede for a moment. It has acquired, inexplicably, a kind of malevolence.

She likes his daughter's play very much, she tells him once he has caught up. It's very generous of him to come.

He wants to ask her what she means by this, but they are at the doorway of a booth now, where the woman in charge of social media tells him to feel free to look around from the entrance, but not to go in. She points out screens, which project the stage below. Crew members run in front of the camera. Bits of music play: loud, then not. What he is seeing is the preparation to stream that afternoon's show on their website, his companion explains. Since mentions of the play had been doing so well on various social media, they thought they should try to broadcast it online. Audience members had become so used to replicating life on a screen thanks to the pandemic, thanks to video calls and home cinema, remote parties and kitchen discos.

To Sophia's father, each black-clad production member is a ghost ensuring his daughter's work haunts the internet. But he nods.

No, that is very good, he concedes, and means it. He tries to override the sudden clench of muscles in his stomach.

18

The tech booth, with its dimmed light and damp smell, has none of the glamour of the rest of the theatre. Rust-coloured carpet has clots of mud and glitter in it; gunmetal and plastic equipment with raised black and red buttons protrudes from everywhere. It is a small, claustrophobic space with him lingering in the doorway. It enables everything. It does not feel right to be in it. He thinks of how beautiful the photos taken by audience members in the light-filled foyer must have been, and how ugly it is in here. On a Tannoy overhead, a woman's voice asks him to take his seat: she tells him the afternoon's performance will begin soon. And dimly, on a Tannoy overhead, Sophia hears a woman's voice asking the theatre's relevant visitors to take their seats. She tells them the afternoon's performance will begin soon.

A strict order of operations governs the theatre's rooftop bar and restaurant. On being seated, its clientele is asked to relay requests to their assigned waiter only, and to wait for said waiter to approach the table before making such requests. It is preferred that customers flag servers down only in the event of an emergency, and otherwise allow staff to attend their allotted tables in accordance with a set rota. It is appreciated that some patience will be involved on behalf of the patrons, but their server will make regular rounds throughout the room, ensuring everyone is seen to as efficiently as possible. In this way, the theatre remains as closely in compliance with government advice as it can. It attempts to prolong the possibility of remaining open.

Sophia listens to the maître d' relay this information as though he finds it delightful to each new set of people arriving around her. She watches one woman tweezer ice out of her drink with her forefinger and thumb, and place it directly on her tongue. The weather is sweat-inducing. London has, uncharacteristically, bestowed perfect summer on a season of misery. Light drapes itself over white sofas and white tables; enhances the view of Covent Garden's glass-roofed market pouring in from windows that fill the wall. In front of her, a menu offers calories but not prices – beef carpaccio or artichoke soup for 400kcal; grilled courgette in saffron butter for 683; a peach melba for 602. Organic coffee or tea served with petit fours, Sophia reads, has no calories but is £6; in a separate slim, hardbound book, a drinks menu offers the same disappointment to a different tune – blood orange bellinis at £18 with no apparent nutritional value. She checks the time on her phone.

Her father is somewhere, three or four floors below. Her father is about to watch her play.

Sophia deals with this thought by watching a man some tables over prise meat out of the clams in his spaghetti vongole. When the maître d' delivers her mother and a small carafe of water to pour into their glasses during the delivery of his ordained servers and rota speech, Sophia's mother interrupts with a request for a large Picpoul. There is a slight pause in the trajectory of the water from the carafe to her glass. Their waiter, he resumes, will be with them momentarily. Sophia watches the impatience on her mother's face shift slowly to boredom and thinks about something her father once said, that: *the only thing missing from your mother's otherwise perfect face is a beak.* It's a terrible sentence, made more terrible by the fact that he said it, and now, in moments like this, it will always live in her head.

In his allocated seat, Sophia's father flicks through his programme. It has advertisements for other plays, interviews with production staff, short stories written by promising young women. Determined to give Sophia a thoughtful, and therefore original, ovation of her work, he avoids summaries of the show. He has come to it blind: he would like to preserve the chance of being pleasantly bowled over by his daughter's talent. He looks instead at rehearsal photos of actors bent earnestly over a script. Sophia is in some of these, holding her cheek in her hand and tipping her head to the side; Sophia is in some of these, wearing a blue button-down shirt and jeans, narrowing her eyes at an older actor. She looks older. She looks completely new to him, and he flicks through the pamphlet hoping to find an image where she smiles. He doesn't know why this should be the case. The last time he gave an interview about a book, the woman he spoke to happened also to be a photographer: she produced a Pentax mid-conversation and taped up a sheet of velvet. It threw him. He'd asked her whether that was intended. Naturally, she'd murmured. She thought his answers had seemed rehearsed. One month later, the paper ran the image, and it was pitiful. The perspective was all wrong. The left side of his face and body looked larger than the right. His eyes were half closed. He'd forgotten to take his glasses off the chain around his neck. They swung askance, wrinkling his shirt. Liver spots on his face.

Everyone else loved it. The paper stuck it online. His publisher said it displayed gravitas.

Nearby, there is a luminous rectangle of white making onerous high-pitched rings: a woman to his right is texting. Not much better in front, where someone is watching, not quietly enough, some kind of film. More staff have been moving fruitlessly up the aisles with signs that warn against taking photos, recording, leaving devices on. It seems impossible for everyone pricking the theatre's intended dusk with the inane remnants of their outside life – email, messenger, weather, news, *Twitter, Twitter, Twitter* – to consider what the situation asks. No phones. Quiet contemplation. You wouldn't play Candy Crush at church. He thinks his neighbour might at least switch her phone off when the dusk around them deepens and the stage flickers blue, but instead there is her elbow jutting upwards and out. Phone aloft. Jerked shutter shot of noise. She has taken a picture. She has the self-consciousness to look appalled, at least; he is smug at the hasty haul of her arms down, and the phone's immediate black. Yet despite himself, he feels pity when he watches her sink back into the chair and look around to see whether she is being judged.

Last night he had resisted logging into his near-defunct Twitter account to see what people were saying about his daughter. The account had been made for him by his agent at the beginning of lockdown on the premise that it would be a way to reconnect with readers in the midst of a difficult time. His agent also suggested he consider sending out a weekly newsletter of stories and anecdotes to people who liked his books. Other authors his age and older were getting good engagement, had been the reasoning that came out of the phone.

Irritated by his agent's statement, Sophia's father had spent a day getting to grips with being on social media. He had checked the profiles of writers he knew, which bore no resemblance to the intelligent, measured people they were. They engaged in a process of constant self-promotion he considered in equal parts exhausting and tasteless to consume – a daily parroting of every good thing papers and strangers said about them with near-identical phrases supplemented above each bit of praise. A single exclamation point; a smiling yellow emoji; the words, *so pleased with this brilliant review*, or else, sandwiched between photos of gardens and daily walks, snippets of their tired pandemic lives; *some news*, which he found particularly despicable. '*Some news*'. The words would appear below an announcement of a new book or a screenshot of a longlist for a prize. Somewhere along the way, Sophia's father had seen an earnest young man declaim that it was his right to post such things, both as a means of self-congratulation, and to raise awareness of his work. Writing was *hard*, it was done in solitude, and when the finished product was released, it drowned in the tides of new-age tech consumerism, which had fucked the attention economy to shreds. The only person he could rely upon to keep his work afloat was him.

All of it was, in total, worse than Facebook.

And yet – who wouldn't feel vulnerable because of it? He hasn't published a book in a decade, but if he had to now, he's unsure how he could do it. In his own heyday, he had known, very well, that his currency lay in caustic-ally quotable remarks made over free drinks about older, venerated authors (declining), world entropy (rising), consumerism (wonderful; unimportant), and sex (inane; hugely important). He would write intelligent novels and make intelligent conversation about them. For a few days in March, he had tried posting links to the articles and reviews he was still writing for other papers. But there was the fact of a strange new paradox between the declining currency of caustic remarks in a market where everyone had become fluent in them and the fact that the only ones of his that got any traction seemed always to be wrong. An article about the death of the male voice in publishing. An old quote about homosexuals and self-flagellation. Suddenly the whole world thought he was a misogynist, that he was against the gays. And of course, he's aware of having been a divisive figure in the past; had leant into it when it meant good money, but this was before his agent had set thousands of strangers up with a direct line of communication to him for their vitriol. He had thought of balancing the scales; honing a man-of-the-people image by telling everyone about his everyday life instead, but the reality was that, other than the temporary visit afforded him by his ex-wife, he lived alone. He depended on the kindness of friends, and the birthday parties they threw for their children; the drinks they suggested on a stray Thursday. He watched the six o'clock news. He struggled to give up smoking. He struggled to feel the inclination to give up smoking. A handful of partners he never felt ready to keep. It may have been true of every other person on the planet, but on the internet, it was somehow not good material for *him* to divulge. He feels helpless and bored, but worse, he still feels, in spite of that, like an idiot. He wants to be able to understand. He makes an effort. He is not a Luddite. He does not feel himself to be a bad or outdated person. He has only just come to his sixties.

In what might have been described as the pinnacle of his career, he had been shortlisted for a prize some critics felt he should have won three books before. His oeuvre contained literary spins on noir and espionage, teenagers having bad sex, cocaine-fuelled language, controversial criticisms on world orders. Merciless, but stylish degradation.

He had lost. His publisher had thrown him a party nonetheless, held in the house of some Swedish millionaire who professed themselves a fan. Around 5 a.m., he had stood in one of their bathrooms and watched his mirror image lick its way down the length of a cloudy blue Rizla, watched the little trail of saliva from its mouth wet the paper. After he had watched it seal the fag with a flourish, seen the catch and spark of a lighter at its chin, he went upstairs and listened to seven different people tell him the book was a masterpiece; that he'd been robbed.

This had not been the point. By that time, he'd had seven novels to his name. He had written them because he had, with a measure of safety induced by the barrier of fiction, wanted to show the world some of his selves. At the very suggestion of dawn, he had eased himself out of the party and gone down the nearby high street. Only the butchers were up: the pig carcasses in the window on their hooks, and their owner by the shop's door, sweeping out the previous night's Camel Light and Marlboro butts from the pavement while pigeons cooed the morning's aubade. In a matter of hours, his agent would email him requests from various radio outlets to discuss the loss. That thought had been in the forefront of his mind when he had climbed into bed at last. He remembers wondering how a person like him should be when they woke up.

None of it bears thinking about. Now, the stage ahead has been curtained off by a semi-transparent black screen and dimly lit, so that the outlines of objects hang in front of the audience, here boxy, here curved. Sophia's father bargains with the heavens, set in carved stone angels and heavy black theatre lights above. *Please, God, let it go well. Give my girl a good flight.*

At half-past two, the auditorium sounds out another celestial prompt for phones to be switched off. When at last the lights overhead dim and the black screen lifts, rows of spectators around and behind him become more apparent. Sophia's father leans forward. It's not what he thought.

Sophia and her mother are negotiating the breadbasket carefully. Their waiter has provided two small plates, silver tongs, a dish of butter, a butter knife. Also, a glass of Picpoul and a negroni. Her mother eyes the sourdough and slides the basket across the table. Sophia places a slice on both plates. She waits for her mother to pick up the butter knife, and watches, instead, her hand grasp the base of the wine glass. Eat, her mother tells her, and Sophia does; she waits for a conversational entry point. After watching her chew for half a minute, Sophia's mother picks up the knife and begins buttering her bread with angular strokes. It, not her daughter, receives the first few words. It hears, left your father's house yesterday – dust all over my couch when I got home – butter too cold; they should serve it at room temp – am I boring you, Sophia?

No, Sophia says. She watches her mother bite into the bread and tries to muster a sense of calm. The sound of her mother's chewing has always been too loud. It sits in perfect contrast to her lifelong reprimands about elbows on tables, posture, napkins over legs.

He's here now, Sophia says. He's watching the matinee.

It seems impossible, but the sound of the chewing gets worse. I'd hoped, her mother swallows, he was watching the evening performance. I thought we were going to have a nice lunch.

This is a talent she has. By nothing more than setting down her bread and saying, *Well?* Sophia's mother has made her daughter wish for an embolism. The waiter comes to ask whether the drinks are all right. Her mother fixes a special smile for him and resumes bringing the temperature of the room down once he has moved on. This is selfish, she says. I've just spent four months patching him up—then reaches into her bag and unpacks its contents onto the table. A compact mirror. A stick of Chanel Rouge Allure. She assembles these around her face, paints her lips the shade Intemporelle 60. Bits of dull peach pigment bleed like spider's legs around her mouth before she catches them with her forefinger and thumb. Sophia remembers copying this gesture in the years she had spent trying to become an adult. She watches her mother apply lipstick so slowly that the silence between them stretches out long enough to turn the notion of an apology into a necessity.

Instead, Sophia picks up the closest coping mechanism she has for dealing with the thought of her father's future displeasure, the reality of which has manifested itself in her mother's puckered mouth. She scrolls. On Instagram, airbrushed women are posting black-and-white photos of themselves with the hashtag 'Challenge Accepted', and accompanying text, which reads, *I am awed by the strength of the women around me.* A little way down, *Glamour* magazine explains the significance of the phenomenon in relation to Turkish femicide via infographics. Her mother allows this for two minutes before she breaks her daughter's focus. Do you expect me to defend you when he comes out? she asks.

Sophia turns her phone over. Her mother's face has dark circles under the eyes, to which she sometimes lifts her fingers in separate turns, like a little curtain going up and down, shielding and revealing them. No, Sophia counters. You don't have to see him. I'm planning to talk to him alone when he comes out. We're going to have dinner. All I want is for you to be nice while we have lunch. I'll be nice back.

Her mother nods. She raises her glass over the table and says, Congratulations on another play. Well done.

After Sophia has put her negroni down, she asks her mother how it feels to have moved back into her own home. Difficult, she tells Sophia. Old things about her house had become newly apparent. The presence of the two bedside tables she had kept in her bedroom, even though she lived alone. The amount of cutlery in the drawers. Second-hand Afghan rugs, which covered scratched floors. It bothered her now, in a way it hadn't previously, that when Sophia's father had moved out all those years ago, he had also freed his time from the constraints of marriage and childcare to earn more money; buy a nicer house. She had ignored this fact while dropping Sophia off as a child over various weekends, kept her eyes squarely on the cups of coffee he offered to be civil, but the past four months spent living with him were enough to discover that in contrast to the plywood shelves she had fitted into her walls, he had teak bookcases. He had more natural light. He had more bedrooms. He had low tables stacked with the evidence of his personal interests – a luxury she had not had time for as a single mother, an aspect of her life she felt was under-developed now. Living with him in his nicer house had, in a way, put the hard-won truce they'd managed to fashion after the marriage had ended on shakier grounds. But only to her. How could she begrudge him now, after twenty years, for living his life without her as he saw fit?

She finishes the last of her wine, waves at their server, who bows his head in acknowledgement and raises one finger as a signal to wait. Sophia grasps at her negroni. You didn't argue about it? she probes.

Not over his house, her mother answers. Not over other things either, really. Your father's usual tactic is to frustrate his opponent into compliance. She watches her daughter flinch in response and veers the conversation to safer ground; says, I've no doubt he'll think you've written something very clever.

You think he won't like it, Sophia snorts.

I didn't tell you he would, her mother points out with alacrity, and surveys her menu. Sophia mimes the same and says, I'm going to have the lemon sole; do you think he won't like it for the same reason you don't? It's really got nothing to do with him.

Her answer gets directed at the menu.

I'm not sure I've ever told you I don't like it – I'm going to have the pork – Anyway, pointless to worry now – Do you think they'll do the potatoes boiled instead of creamed if I ask?

The latter sentence is a contribution to an ongoing argument, broached whenever Sophia and her mother eat together at a restaurant. Her mother asks the kitchen to offer items that are not available, and Sophia tells her this is not the way the world works: that it is unreasonable to expect people to turn on her whim. Why don't you have the aubergine, she interposes, with black rice instead?

Now her mother chews an invisible wad of gum while she looks at the menu. I have a rule, she says eventually, not that you'd know, about not prying into your relationship with your father. I think it's fair. I decided early on my responsibility was to let you make your own mind up about him, separate to whatever I felt. You – she looks up from her menu – are breaking the rules of engagement. She watches her daughter's face pinken; slip behind her grown-up drink with its lucent orange wedge.

ONE:
THE MAN ONSTAGE IS WEARING
A PURPLE PAISLEY SHIRT

A line from Sophia's play:
— *You laugh like a man.*

A line from Sophia's play:
— *Fucker.*

A line from Sophia's play:
— *Yes. Now we've observed the most important things about each other.*

He doesn't know where the dialogue is coming from, but it barely registers while he takes in the set. Sophia has it almost exact to the place they stayed in Sicily. She had finished school, and he thought it fitting to take her to Europe before her first term of university started. Not a grand tour, exactly, but close enough. He thought she could help him write his new book.

He thinks she must have used photos to replicate everything; no memory could be so loyal. There are details he hasn't thought of in years, and which come back now

– a chequerboard of tiles low on each kitchen wall, and mosaic ones around various rudimentary appliances: oven, washing machine, fridge, sink. She has done justice to the enormous size of the wooden back door and the almost comically contrasting small windows done with crude latticework. Beautiful, round marble table he is conversant with and still dreams of. He is glad she dreams of it, too. Then its array of stuff: bowls of parsley, dill, oranges, eggs, sugar; papers stacked round like a wedge of geese; mocha pot; constant coffee cups, espresso mugs, stray plates, stray knives, stray forks, stray pens, and around the clutter, light, netted chairs. Nooks stuffed with iron pans and woven bowls; photos of strangers and saints dotted about with Blu Tack and Sellotape. Silver ladles on silver hooks. It was a very good place to be, not just to work. Coming down for breakfast each morning turned into a process of ceremonials that could never be mustered in England: rising heat, smell of herbs, fresh ricotta to eat, and salt on the lips dropped down from their sweating cupids' bows. The rest of the house had been charming enough, but Sophia liked the kitchen so much he had agreed to work in it when she asked. He could see her point.

An overhead bulb slowly brightens, throws more light onstage. The windows remain dark. So, in the play, he reasons, it is night.

He has his own recollections of the holiday: they come to him now. Sophia late in the day of being seventeen, Sophia at the cusp of adulthood, was the daughter he could begin to make smart, boisterous conversation with. Up to that time they had only been together during weekends. Over the years, he had tried very hard to do things that would give continuity to the between times of seeing each other – gave her copies of books he was reading so that she could carry them in her bag and they might turn the same pages during weekdays. He noted down bits of school gossip she'd told him after leaving his flat on Sunday nights and tracked each plot as it evolved; taught her how to carry off jokes with swear words, and then awaited the report on how these things had been received by her friends. The result was good: she only rolled her eyes at him for fun. There was, between them, affectionate seriousness. All of this, he'd hoped, would buoy a summer together, mitigate the fact that it would be the longest stretch of time they'd spend under the same roof after his divorce.

And so – 2010. Aeolian Islands. They'd taken a plane from London to Sicily; from there, sailed first on a ferry and then on a small white boat that rocked like a bell towards a catalogue of blistered cliff faces. The motion of it had been so back and forth he was unsure they'd ever arrive. Sophia's teeth shone out from her face. She was not made nauseous by the sea the way he was. When the boat tipped more in one direction than the other, she threw her body exaggeratedly with it in glee, then threw her body back, incandescent and intact. Such were the little vibrations she made all through their first days there, despite the island's oppressive heat. Then hours a day in which he spoke, and she, as his amanuensis, made words appear in response. The clack of keys as she transmitted his cadence into a machine. Her low voice reading printed sheets back to him. Soft glide of his pencil correcting her more creative decisions.

The dialogue from offstage grows closer. Two figures enter from the right. One is a woman in something that doesn't have enough fabric to be called a dress. Another is

37

a man, halfway through the process of taking off his shirt. It happens so quickly the shirt might not have been there at all – purple fabric gets dashed across the stage with choreographed haphazardness onto the floor.

It's not how he remembers the kitchen being used. It jars him to think that she would imagine strangers there. The house was a familiar place to him: the summer retreat of a friend who invited Sophia's father regularly as a thank you for introducing him to his wife. The couple would host him once a year for two weeks. It had been a ritual. At that point he was already separated from Sophia's mother, and this fact had created a desire to witness the happy domesticity his shrewd, albeit mildly tipsy, instinct had wrought. He watched them quarrel affectionately over dinners and lunches. When they had had their first child, he'd asked about town until he found a local woman with charmingly poor English to help maintain the house for the four months of their stay. He got on particularly well with her; in her presence, he was not the only outsider. She was older than him by ten years or so, but spry, and delighted by his bad Italian, which she corrected between cackles or swats of her tea towel. It brought back the childhood feeling of flirting with matron, more for the sake of entertainment than anything else. When he had confided that he felt the house would be the perfect place to spend time with Sophia, his friend understood; said, Yes. It's a happy home.

But onstage, the man staggers, pushes the woman in a minidress into the kitchen table. Sound of splitting porcelain. A bowl breaks like this every night. Oranges shudder and heave themselves around the floor. It means the eggs are in question, too, dish sliding further towards the table's

38

edge, their shells in threat. There begins an audible exchange of saliva through mics.

The actors are expert – have practised the pitch of their laughs, and the exact moment at which her breasts should come out of the dress's top. There's a touch of purposefully bad cinema about the way their hands grasp through hair until they find scalp. But the indistinct glow of the play's lighting and the tasteful décor that makes up the set gives these proceedings depth; bestow the gaucheness with a degree of majesty as well. When he makes a step, her leg knots under his and moves, too, in tango. When she bares her teeth on his shoulder, his throat, it is terrible – but the reddened flesh of her lips comes away unsmeared and remains beautiful.

Sophia's father makes quick work of rearranging his expectations. Mostly, this happens on autopilot – because, yes, now that he thinks of it, he had brought a handful of women back to the house. But quietly so. And his daughter, while not actively immersed in the specifics of his post-marital life, hardly thought of him as a virgin. He had, however, hoped that she'd thought of him as fatherly during the time they'd shared on holiday. He is not sure whether he is supposed to be watching himself or not.

Two thoughts keep his back from sagging. He'd never fucked anyone in the kitchen, loudly or otherwise. And the actor bears no resemblance to him. The actress does, he has to admit, look a little like a companion he'd met while he and Sophia had been on holiday. It's disconcerting, in the sense that he can't imagine how his daughter would know that she'd had short, dark hair and a washboard for a chest. But, he reasons delicately against the horror that Sophia might have watched him where he did not wish to be seen, there were many small-breasted brunettes in the world. He considers an unhappy coincidence in casting and distracts himself with the thought of a different woman he'd met, one or two weeks into their time abroad.

Sophia hadn't been there, he's sure. Happy with her work on his novel, he'd indulged his daughter's requests to take control of the bottle of fortified wine he'd opened after dinner. Sophia, usually equipped with a good head on her shoulders when it came to drinking, had not accounted for the heat. Four dessert glasses in, she folded fast. It's possible, he thinks, that if they'd got tipsy at the same speed, he might have taken her along into town. But as it was, he had not been confident enough in his parental authority to guide his giddy, occasionally hiccuping daughter along loose cobblestones; to shush the laughs that rocketed out of her. At the point where she had turned boisterous, rude, even, he had tucked her into bed and gone out on his own. He remembers calling his ex-wife before he left to seek her approval at this decision. She'd scolded him for letting Sophia get drunk. Looking at the stage now, he feels the shame he couldn't muster ten years ago.

In town, he had settled himself nicely at a small pine-built bar and found himself able to make conversation with the man in his mid-twenties pouring his shots. Some Italians spoke better English than the English: this was one. He can remember telling him about his work despite the interludes in which the man had to serve someone else. He remembers the question: what do you write about? And his reply – Women, always, women. There was no need to explain why. The bartender seemed to know. And being a writer, he'd then asked, does that make you attractive to women?

40

Answer: No. He picked up his drink. That was shaky territory. He remembers warmth blowing onto his face: his laugh circling the drain of his glass and coming back up to meet him.

Then his companion had moved away to settle someone else's tab. He thinks this is the moment he met Susanna, although now it seems rather neat, even to him. But given where he has found himself, in this theatre, he allows a degree of fantasy. It makes sitting in his chair more enjoyable – there's a light ache in the small of his back. His thighs are going numb. There's no harm in remaining convinced that she had overheard, leant over and said, So, you're carrying out important work?

Yes, he'd answered, I am.

That's funny, Susanna said. I thought I heard you were writing a book.

On account of that he'd bought her a drink.

He can't quite tell what Sophia means by setting up a sex scene in the only place she's ever, as far as he knows, engaged with his writing. It feels uncomfortable. True, he's written enough filth of his own, though it mostly centred the preamble and the aftermath. Mainly, it served as a way of conveying humour, impotence, cruelty or carnage. In his version of events, both parties would be made to look used, or ridiculous, or wrong, or dissatisfied. Sophia's seems more like an enactment of the criticisms that are levelled at his work. Only one of the people his daughter has put onstage looks like they're doing something wrong.

That night in Italy, Susanna had been the one who was inquiring, imperious. She'd examined him down the length of her cigarette. She'd seemed a few drinks ahead of him, and so, compelled by good British manners, he had ordered more alcohol until he felt himself to be equally oiled. He had let her steer the conversation towards topics she could argue furiously over with him, namely her dissatisfaction with the Italian government; then-recent leaks by an Australian whistle-blower regarding the war in Afghanistan; the inability of the English to produce good coffee or wine.

The comfort in reviving this time, years ago, is how much better he looked. At the start of the last decade, he knew he still had the vestigial trace of something that could have been called handsomeness. Only the beginnings of pockets under his eyes. Only the faint trace of hair from his ears; in his nose. Less skin that sagged around the arms and torso. These days, he is not completely gone, but it is apparent to him now in a way it wasn't then: he will be, soon. Neither of the two women he is sitting close to have looked at him with any sort of warmth or desire. There is enough sweat, and nudity, and lust in the room to observe. They are watching the push–pull of the actors on-stage. They are watching, he supposes, other things as well; imparting meaning into gesture until the physical becomes allegory. Rightly or wrongly, the assumptions they will make concern various assertions of dominance and gender norms: how the man covers his partner's face with his hand. How the woman's moans muffle in response. How her nudity seems greater than his. Around Sophia's father, an entire theatre becomes expert in the art of semiotics and porn.

Too much is going on inside his head. Memories are blooming and ebbing faster than what's happening onstage. The disjunct in tempo, the difficulty in knowing which image to attend to, real or recalled, makes him clumsy. He would atone for this fact, too, except he's sure of it, he's sure – the shirt the actor flung so extravagantly on the floor is a carbon copy of one he has hanging in his wardrobe.

(When Sophia's father had finished with Susanna, she'd wandered off the sofa in search of water. He had seen her in the kitchen, naked, running the tap, cupping her palms under it and raising them to her mouth. She'd touched the oranges in their bowl; the PG Tips he had brought from home. The house hadn't come with a kettle – he boiled water in a pan and poured it over a teabag for her. He remembers feeling quite touched by her lifting the mug to his lips instead until he drank; by her peeling rind off fruit and eating noiselessly. She had been very good about his request for them to be quiet. He remembers embracing her back on the sofa. She'd turned to look up at him, roguish, and asked: In the morning, are you going to yearn for me? He'd smiled at her, kissed her nose and said, No. Probably not. Not long after, she'd plucked a few more teabags and oranges from his kitchen, and he'd given her a bag for them before he watched her go out the back door.)

I'm going to tell a white lie, Sophia's mother says, and smiles graciously across the room at their waiter. At his next scheduled appearance, she proffers him the menu. All of the potatoes, she points out, are made with butter and cream, which is a dietary concern. He nods seriously, suggests asking the kitchen whether they could substitute with dairy-free alternatives. To Sophia's surprise, her mother carries off a look of gentle modesty like a magic trick. A note is made for the potatoes to be boiled and mixed with whatever herbs the kitchen thinks will work best. You should be onstage, Sophia says after he has left. Momentarily, her mother's eyes close. I don't think, she murmurs, I need to perform another act as your father's love interest.

Sophia prepares to extend another apology across the table. She says, No, of course, how thoughtless, and imagines the words 'I'm sorry' travelling from her to her mother like a salt shaker several times over until all her verbal missteps have suitably intensified, enhanced their general conversation. Tell me, she offers instead, why you stayed with him over lockdown for so long.

Yes. Her mother's shoulders readjust. She begins fiddling with her wine glass in quarter-turns. Sophia watches it go round. At first, her mother explains, she had meant to stay for a week, and then a week and a half, then two weeks, then two and a half. Put like that, it hadn't ever seemed like she was going to stay for very long. She had been counting forward in time, not back.

The initial stretch had been difficult work. He'd never been especially good at housework, but he had never been a slob. When she arrived, she found he'd stopped doing the dishes. He'd stopped doing laundry. He kept the TV on at all hours, a trait she had never associated with him before, and although she was familiar with his habit of muttering to himself whenever he was on the go, the way he did it now had become troublesome: he would sit on the sofa and stare into space while his lips moved.

Between the process of washing his clothes, opening his curtains, and scrubbing the kitchen stove, she set to work on him. Most of what he'd needed had been company, and for both their sakes, she tried very hard to work out the line between companionship and coddling. In truth, it only blurred because she had also been laundering his socks; suggesting in the mildest of tones that he might feel better after a bath. But once the house was clean, all it took was a few hours of conversation a day, scattered between breakfast and supper. He hadn't needed physical care.

I understand, Sophia ventures. You were there to help his mental health.

Well, I was there because I was worried he was sad, her mother says. Sophia looks at her, amused. She waits for more. Her mother clarifies. The reason she had showed up at his house at all was a phone call in which he had been barely coherent. Without so much as a 'hello', he had launched into a speech that, as far as she could make out, was about the rudeness of the man who ran his local corner shop. She'd listened to this patiently for half an hour, but the moment she tried to bring the conversation to a close, he'd burst into tears.

She'd never heard him cry before. It was so unusual that the only rational response, at the time, had been to throw whatever she could into a bag and go. She looks up.

Was he depressed? Sophia asks.

I don't know, her mother says. He was just down. It was a difficult time to be alone; everyone felt down. Didn't you? She watches her daughter's hand rest lightly on her phone. That's why I'm asking, Sophia responds. There was a large-scale dip in mental health across the country when lockdown hit, and it wasn't uncommon for people to end up depressed. Did you find him a therapist? Did you get him medication? He has healthcare.

Oh for God's sake, her mother collapses. He was sad because he was alone, so I went to keep him company – which meant he wasn't alone, so he stopped being sad. It's very simple. I doubt your father, out of anyone on earth, needs more drugs inside of him. He'd already had enough for two lifetimes when he hit thirty.

No, Mum, Sophia explains. Sertraline isn't coke.

Everything she has heard has made her feel worse. By now, her father will undoubtably have recognised the set onstage. The thought of him now as unhappy and bowed settles in her stomach like flu.

The first place she'd written about the house they stayed in was in her diary, not her play, the morning after they'd arrived. It had been wide. The floors were stone-tiled,

47

geometric and cold to walk on. White walls with nothing on them where sometimes arches appeared. Each time she found a new one she moved to slot her body into each alcove. The furnishings themselves were sparse, but full of *stuff* – jugs, trays, plants. Despite the busyness of various patterned surfaces, she'd felt that something was missing from it. Plainly, it was a holiday home. It felt like a transitory place. She'd made notes about the kitchen: it had brown and white tiles like chocolate Battenberg. Her father had not been there when Elena had walked in.

For a moment they'd appraised each other. Elena had introduced herself by name and Sophia observed a crest of brown fringe over a beaky face, the face made glamorous with tar-black eyelashes and blue eyeshadow. A long, flowery wrap dress on a thin, wrinkled body that sagged at the arms. Shopping bags at their end. A netted bag full of oranges.

What Elena must have seen was a seventeen-year-old girl with her nose close to her paper and pen, in a bikini top and rolled-up cotton shorts. The awkwardness, when strangers meet and are unsure of each other's purpose. When Sophia finally thought of something to say, she remembers her father breezing in, shirt open. She remembers him catching Elena immediately, laughing, *Ah, buongiorno! Buongiorno!* – before kissing the top of Sophia's head. Then he took two shopping bags from the woman's arms, leaving her with one.

Elena will help us while we're here, had been the explanation while Elena unearthed something wrapped in white paper. The tang of fish went into the fridge. Sophia, uncertain, had smiled. It had looked like they knew each other. When her father began putting herbs in a bowl

48

already loaded with eggs, there was an ease with which Elena had batted his hand away and plucked them out; prefixed his name with *Mister* and said, *No, solo uova, uova*. He did not look perturbed. With casual charm, he gave way and in slow Italian repeated, *Ah, solo uova, of course: sono il tuo schiavo* – and moved out of the way for her to fix what he'd done. The herbs went into another bowl, next to one with oranges. *You see, Sophia*, he'd said. *We were starving and now, thanks to Elena, we're full to the brim*. Then, catching the notebook, *What's that you've got there?* She'd removed it before it could catch his grasp and excused herself for a walk.

You look worried, Sophia's mother says. Her daughter has gone pallid in the restaurant.

(For the duration of her walk, Sophia had tucked her note-book into the waistband at the back of her shorts, something she had seen her father do as though his writing gear was a gun. Because of the position of the house, directly by the beachfront, the first impression had not been heat, nor the peeling pink walls of other buildings adjacent. Every-thing was sound, sound – the tide's white noise rasping closer, then withdrawn, the maracas of pebbles being disturbed.

Sophia took the road by its incline. Dappled bits of sun shone everywhere, truer than any sun she'd seen before: richer and golder. Sometimes dishcloths hung above her, suspended on plastic-coated rows of string – blue and white linen against blue and white sky. On the main road, there was a man in a pale-yellow shirt with thick, curling hair. When he went into a nearby café, Sophia followed.

It had been a gelateria. Through the windows, she watched him banter with the owner of the shop, point-ing at frozen clouds of pastel cream contained in their stainless-steel tubs. She'd blushed at the realisation that she had no Italian to parse with him, and that the owner of the shop had very little, if any, English to offer. Instead, through concerted smiles and nods, the two men helped her pick out four scoops of almond and melon gelato served in a cup wrapped with paper and topped with cream.

Sophia remembers taking her dessert outside the shop and sitting with her back to the street, arranging her hair and eating slowly so that when the man walked out again, she could show him how much she was enjoying the ice cream and thank him. She had liked the dimple in his chin. She waited.

When he passed by the table Sophia smiled. He noticed, nodded once, looked away.

It had all been so much more solitary than she'd fore-seen. She got lost on the way home: ended up at a store selling knock-off Nike trainers and sports bras which maintained its own precise sense of kitsch next to a wine bar done in dark wood with a bottle-green canopy. Sophia had noticed this and liked it but feared forgetting. There'd been no one to tell or help witness, and there was no way to wield her camera's phone that did not turn everything around her too bright, too flat. All the nuance went out of it. She'd tried anyway, there already being an album on Facebook reserved for what had been termed 'Summer '10'. Yet, small irritants had emerged. Dirt. Slow walkers. Her hairline and shoulders had begun to burn. At another store where everything seemed to be marked 50 per cent off, she'd looked through a crate of straw hats, all alike and yet imperfect through the small differences that existed between them. She looked at them for twenty minutes, aware that they were, in essence, the same, until her temper broke and she left, uncovered and burning as before. It had taken forty minutes to find her way back to the house.)

After almost a month of staying with him, her mother continues, the point at which the government had announced a conditional plan for people returning to work, Sophia's father had improved. You may have noticed, she says, the progression between your first video call and successive ones. Then again, perhaps not. The contradiction of the time had been the heightened moral obligation to consider other people as a means to keeping one's own self-interest afloat. Showing other people care meant avoiding them. It's the best excuse you've ever had, Sophia's mother laughs, for not seeing us.

Sophia bites a hangnail on her right hand. By May he was better, she prompts.

Her mother nods. Much better. It had been easy to measure his well-being against the amount of time she had to herself. Eventually, it had been possible to stop thinking of staying there as a sacrifice: she had time to read, to prune the grape vines in his garden. There had been what she now thought of as a golden period in which he became her host. He started buying food again. He poured her a glass of wine in the evening, and when she thanked him, he said, *it's the least I can do.* For most of the day, he left her to her own devices. Her prompts for him to shower or do laundry became unnecessary. That stage had been buoyed by the novelty of his gratitude to her. She had been able to relax. Leaving then would have only caused them both to be alone, still unsure of their ability to safely revert to the friends and diversions that made up their separate lives before. Staying, while things had been going well, meant the quiet comfort of another body close by.

I couldn't tell you why we didn't continue in that vein. Sophia's mother frowns. But she had found him in the living room one afternoon, watching a comedian on the television. She couldn't remember his name now, but the defining act of his career had been masturbating in front of several different women.

Sophia knows immediately the person being discussed. She tells her mother. Her mother grimaces. That one, she says. Yes. It wasn't nice to see your father laughing at his jokes. A lot of them were about hating childcare; about how degrading it felt to be in love, to approach women for love, or sex. And I'd read a lot about this comedian when those women came forward to say what happened. I think the stand-up your father was watching had been filmed before those allegations had been made, but the jokes were still vulgar. They didn't point directly to his wrongs, but they were in character, if you see what I mean.

I didn't like the fact that he could watch the show so easily, she says, but it's none of my business what your father enjoys in his spare time. It was his house, after all. And I'd forgotten how different we were from each other. But either way, I sat myself next to him and whenever a bad joke came up and I'd say, *I don't understand. I'm not sure why you laughed.* I tried to ask whether the jokes didn't register differently with the knowledge of what the comedian had done. I'd like to think that my aim at the time was to give your father the benefit of the doubt: perhaps he'd caught onto something I hadn't. Perhaps I *had* misunderstood. Your father seemed to have real pity for this man, for how pathetic his desires were. He kept referring to the fact that the comedian had asked each of these women whether masturbating in front of them was okay.

Sophia attempts to overcome her impatience with her mother. *How does anyone misunderstand their own opinion?* she points out.

You know, you have a freedom you're not aware of, her mother tells her abruptly. What would you have said to him?

She watches Sophia brush breadcrumbs from the table-cloth before them, seemingly unaware of the mess she is transferring onto the floor. She listens to her daughter speak of the relationship between power, and money, and consent. When Sophia is done, she shakes her head.

But your father's mind doesn't work like that, she says. He has a tendency towards excessive sympathy. He doesn't like inconsistent logic. He would say, you either give consent, or you don't. In fact, he asked me to agree that it was possible to feel unhappy or uncomfortable with a scenario despite having agreed to the conditions that enabled it.

You didn't, Sophia grimaces.

I did, her mother says. I told him, *that's how I felt about our marriage.* And it still is, to some extent. It's a waste in my life.

Her daughter looks at the floor. You had me, she says.

Sophia's mother makes a conscious effort to relax. This

is a question Sophia has asked her again and again over time. Only the language has changed. At twelve years old, the question was, *If you love me, that means you love Dad.* At sixteen, *But if you hadn't married him, I wouldn't be here.* She has tried to answer honestly when it appeared. She has tried to give credence to two competing narratives. Her daughter has never liked this. I had you, Sophia's mother tries to affirm.

It doesn't work. The origin of their conversation spills over. The words should sound gentle, but she is not in a gentle mood. Well, I realised it was an unfair thing to say to him anyway, she hurries on. It escalated the conversation past friendly chat. He was talking about Hollywood, and I was taking shots at our marriage. And the terrible thing, I remember, was that he kept telling me I was treating the women we were discussing as though they had no agency. I might have been. His argument seemed to rest on his ability to endow the women we were discussing with more power than I felt they had: to say what they felt, to do as they liked.

But he was wrong, Sophia says.

That's immaterial. Her mother frowns. By that point I'd blurred the lines. The conversation became pointed enough to feel he was talking about me. I had to live with him, Sophia. I made peace. Not that it worked.

Here, Sophia says a number of cruel things to her mother in a calm tone of voice. She calls her an enabler. She calls her a coward. She tells her she has compromised her beliefs for comfort. She asks whether her mother understands that she is defending the very behaviour that had made her marriage untenable. Her mother interjects. She says, I'm telling you why I was upset because you asked to hear it.

Sophia does not relent, explains that she is merely trying to point to the root cause of the relayed distress, that her mother would be happier in the long run if she stuck to her convictions. This tips things over the edge. *You're just like him*, her mother barks. You're doing exactly what he does. I tell you something you don't like, and you bull your way through until I roll over. You just know what you want to do, and then you do it, without thinking of others.

Sophia is not without shame. She excuses herself from the table.

Now the stage floor. Sophia's father examines the discarded purple shirt. He recalls a weekend in the early stages of parenthood. At the time, Sophia had been old enough to understand what he did and young enough to ask him unending questions about how things worked. She had subjected her father to an inquiry about his job. She'd been nothing short of forensic, and he had not spared her any customary abbreviation to suit her status as a child.

Daddy, how do you make a book?

The sound of pretend sex punctures these precious thoughts. He thinks he told her, Usually, one gets stuck on an idea they've seen enacted in real life and they imagine a story to explain how it may or may not make sense. He thinks Sophia asked, *What's 'enacted'?*

It means when knowledge or thought or feeling is portrayed in definite terms or action. For example, you might 'enact' being angry by *shouting*. He had tickled her stomach and shouted the word 'shouting'. When she had finished laughing, her face turned serious once more.

How do you imagine a story?

It's amazing, really, how perfectly rendered the actor's

shirt is. He wants to walk onstage and pick it up; he wants to take it home, and place it safely in his wardrobe where it belongs. He's not sure he's ever gone to bed with a woman as loud as the actress onstage. He wishes he could shush her.

No stories are entirely imaginary, cherub, he'd said then. Everything is always a little bit real. Sometimes you steal things from other stories and change them until they work how you like.

Her brow had remained confused. It's very similar to when you play with your toys, he told her.

Am I imagining a story with my toys?

Yes, that's exactly what you do.

Sophia had considered this new information by sitting up very straight, and when her lips slowly compressed into an anxious, horizontal little line, he wondered with suppressed glee whether he had just handed her information that would change the trajectory of her life. At her next sentence – *Then I can make a book, too* – he made his back as straight as hers. If you want, he told her. She stuck out her tongue. He did it, too.

What, she had said, depositing the little roll of pink back into her mouth, *should I make a book about?*

All the things you think about a lot. You can write them down as if they were happening to your toys.

She'd nodded, announced, *I know what I'm going to do.* He'd given her a pencil and three sheets of lined A4, but she had shaken her head. *I want it to look like that.* She'd pointed at the hardback books on his shelf. After he had explained that she would first have to do a rough draft on ordinary paper in order to have something to eventually print as a book, that it would take a long time to produce something good, she had laughed and asked for lunch. The glee he'd felt had subsided.

In the theatre's dark, he weighs up what to do out of love. There have been enough divergences so far for him to believe that Sophia's play is a self-contained thing that may only tangentially concern him. He measures how much work he can get the words 'based on' to do. He keeps imagining the production staff nestled at peripheries of various borders, filming; the staging assistants preparing to move in fluid lines, removing props, adding others; each human silhouette made less perceptible with black bandanas on their face. One thing he has not been able to get out of his mind is the phone being clasped by the woman to his right. He feels, very strongly, it should not be in the theatre. It should not be anywhere near this play about his life. When he finds himself leaning unconsciously towards it as though to remove it from her hand, she leans back and withdraws it into her seat.

And in the ornate bathroom outside the theatre's restaurant, Sophia locks a stall door and, still standing, cries. She remembers returning from her first walk alone in Sicily; coming back to the house to find that Elena had gone. Only her father remained, still in the kitchen, drinking coffee, smoking. He'd looked up as though she'd only been gone for five minutes and said, Breakfast?

Sophia had eyed the clock on the kitchen's southern wall. Late breakfast, she smiled.

Late breakfast. The oranges in their bowl. The cereal, the soft-boiled eggs; Bialetti coffee pot on the table between them. He'd read Austen while she dipped macine into a bowl of milk. Eventually absent-minded questions began, did their back and forth across the table.

Where did you go? I don't know. There were a lot of shops. *Sophia*, with the 'a' drawn out. *There are volcanoes and castles here.* There are castles at home, and you hate those. *No volcanoes, though.* Sophia had said, Hm, and picked at her nails.

Did you buy anything? he'd asked. Gelato, she replied. *Chocolate?* No, melon.

And with real pride, he'd breathed, *Oh, good girl.*

Thanks. *Seen any fetching young men?*

She had crossed her legs.

Obviously not, Dad.

He'd looked over his book at her, an eyebrow raised. Then – *You'll need more clothes on the next time you go for a walk.* He'd put the book down. *Have you called your mum?* No. Have you? *No.* The conspirator's glance between father and child before he'd said, *Well, let's get to it then.*

Sophia had taken the silverware and plates to the sink; he'd brought a laptop to the table and opened it to a word processor. She'd sat before it, and her father had remained standing. He'd put a hand on her shoulder and rubbed it lightly. Then, Sophia supposed it could have meant several things. A signal to preparation, gratitude, parental pride – it settled her into her chair and poised her back straight for work. But after that she had not been his daughter anymore. The voice that issued came sharp, and only half aware of her presence. It said, *You'll take down everything I say exactly as I say it. If I say new paragraph, start a new paragraph. If I say comma, add a comma. When I ask you to read something back to me, you'll do it in the same style, noting any punctuation that occurs. Occasionally I might ask you to strike through; do you know how to do that on there? Good.* He'd picked up his copy of Austen. *Let's do a test run with this. Type as I read:*

Go slowly, please, said Sophia.

Half a minute had passed before she brought him to a halt.

Clearer, she'd said, and at his look of annoyance, told him, You said it had to be a team effort before we came here. She'd registered the disturbance across his face, replicated in his voice when he said, *What do you mean by 'clearer'?*

You're talking to yourself, not to me. *Well, I am to some extent,* he'd argued. *That's how it's meant to be. Your job is to take it all down so that I can talk freely. That way we come out with a draft for me to edit in good time.* Okay, Sophia had said. But I need you to address me. I'm worried I'll miss things if I feel like you're not talking to me.

Don't be difficult, Sophia. We're only practising. Read the last line back to me.

She had.

Quite so, her father had said. *New paragraph open quote start italics—*

When you say start italics—

The following in italics, now go again—

With her neck bobbing between the screen and his voice, she'd seen him move towards one of the kitchen cabinets, book still in hand. The reading had continued without pause while he'd extracted a glass and filled it at the sink. He'd said, *New paragraph,* and drank deeply; refilled the glass again, and went on—

Open quote and start italics—

she'd felt the beginnings of a headache—

close italics—

he'd started making little circles in the air as he drew to a close; she'd never seen him do anything like it before—

full stop, new paragraph, indent—

she'd wondered whether he would forgive her if she asked him to stop; if she decided that, in the end, she simply wanted a holiday to find out whether she liked cigarettes and the look of herself tanned, because there was such a lack of excitement in all the things she ever did—

And then he'd turned back and become her father again: there, saying,

Full stop end quote—
—smiling,
—tender,
again.

In the bathroom stall, Sophia wonders whether he'd been aware of how quickly he made the switch. He'd said – *Well, poppet? Let's see how you've done* – so warmly. And for that reason it had been so easy to let him slide the laptop over and turn the screen away.

Oh, very good, he'd approved. *You see? It's not at all hard.*

This is how you want it? she'd asked.

Yes. That's exactly how it should be from start to finish.

Would you, Sophia had tried, mind sitting down while I type? It earned her a thin smile.

Before he began to pace again he'd cut up an orange. She watched him put it on a plate in front of her, where ten smiling crescents either rocked on their peel or lay flat and glistened sickly. *Snack if you need it* was the explanation.

It took hours. When they finished, he'd insisted they print all the pages she'd typed and go over the afternoon's work. The printer had been on the bottom of a two-tier side table in the living room, hidden under a cloth that covered the surface as a whole. Someone, Sophia cannot remember who, had placed fresh flowers in a vase on top. Next to them was a telephone. Her father had lifted the glass tube with its stalks and its water and used the weight of it to hold the fold of fabric he'd pushed back in order to access the machine.

She'd worried about the creases he was creating in the material. The laptop's hot, laboured wheeze coming out of the fan onto her arm had hurt – there'd been no paper in the printer; and her father was vigorous in his search.

Everything he moved became incrementally messier than before; became touched. We're ruining this house, Sophia had thought.

When the paper was found at last, the laptop had left marks on her skin; raised blots. She looks at her arms now, in the theatre's bathroom. Nothing red, or angry. As though it had never happened.

Her father had sat on the floor while the printer coughed their work out. It seemed never-ending. Each time a new page slid from the metal roller, he'd caught it and added it to the growing pile by rapping the sheets against the stone floor until they came together, uniform. He would look up at her and nod, as though they were surgeons trading swabs and scalpels in a theatre, the guttering printer giving birth, and Sophia, when she thinks of this, recalls realising – no, it did not make a difference whether she was sitting and he was standing, or she was up and he was down. In their scenario, those positions could only have one outcome.

Back at the kitchen table, her father had patted himself down until he had produced both a cigarette and a pencil. The first, he'd stuck in his mouth. The second, he'd handed to her. Sophia had been surprised. She'd thought that printing would mean they'd finish for the day: that they might start having fun. *Read*, he'd said. *Punctuation and all.*

He never said please for the duration of their work together.

The times she had read to him before in her life had happened years ago, as homework. Her school sent her home with a crudely stapled handmade notebook that said, 'Reading Journal'. Inside, four columns demanded the demarcation of date, book, comment, and signature. These assigned readings usually happened over the weekend – her father was her audience. He heard her mispronounce words she'd never read and then gently sounded them out for her; accompanied his corrections with etymologies she would nod seriously at and then forget. The results were always glowing. Her father was prone to punctuating statements like 'Sophia reads so well' with exclamation marks in the comment column. The school she had attended used colours to denote various levels of reading ability. When the notebooks she brought home changed from yellow to blue, from blue to red, and red to purple, he gave her extra dessert on Fridays.

Introduction, Sophia had read. He'd frowned.

What about the date?

I don't think you gave me a date to write down.

Reprovingly – *Sophia* . . .

Her impulse to argue, even then. She remembers springing to clear herself of this injustice, crying, You didn't give me a date to write down.

But worse than an argument, condescension. He handed her the date sternly, again. She wrote it down. She felt the sunburn on her shoulders prickle.

At five in the afternoon, she'd put her pencil down. The glutinous heat of the air. Her father left the kitchen briefly to put the manuscript away, and she'd held her face in her hands. It had seemed so distressing: that she had not had the chance to transfer the morning's pictures from her phone onto her laptop and put them on Facebook for her friends. Then there had been the soft sliding sound of palms rubbing together and then coming apart, the sound of orange peels falling into the bin. Her father, extending a hand with exaggerated theatricality and saying, *Madame.* He'd led her graciously to the fridge where he produced two aubergines and a bottle of fortified wine. He'd said, *All right, you worked well. You can have a glass so long as you do the chopping.* A small win. But she remembers drinking too quickly, and the chuckle he produced as he refilled the glass each time without comment. It had taken the entirety of the time they did the dishes in to clear her head enough to ask, May I be excused, please?

He said, *When I was your age I was outside, getting lots of fresh air. Come to town with me.* Sophia had looked at him, dully. The wine, perhaps, or the kitchen table, had sharpened her instinct for cruelty. She pointed at the laptop. It probably would serve her better to spend time away from screens. He had smiled. *It would, it would.* Sophia had raised her eyebrows. She said, I think I've been bored by you enough for today.

And he had told her that she was drunk. He had told her to go to bed.

A line from Sophia's play:
— *Would you like a cigarette?*

A line from Sophia's play:
— *No. I'm always meaning to quit, aren't you?*

A line from Sophia's play:
— *I don't think so. The body accepts its daily increments of harm.*

It's like cocktail-party conversation, Sophia's father thinks. It makes absolutely no sense.

Onstage, the actor finishes smoking, and the obvious thud of a bedframe hitting a wall resumes, again and again. After the two actors had finished their prolonged build-up to sex, the upper section of the kitchen's high back wall had revealed itself as a partition; lifted, introduced a new set. It was impressively done. The new set looked nothing like the kitchen: it was a white box containing a white bed and nothing else. From somewhere, a smoke machine misted the area with soft vapour.

At first Sophia's father hadn't been sure of the intent. The new part of the stage looked like heaven compared to the gnarled wood, the clutter it sat above. But now that he has been watching the two actors fucking in it for almost ten minutes, it looks unreal. It looks like a new-age porn set.

His first honest thought had been that a sex scene this prolonged was a brilliant device to kick off a play with. It was the sort of move that gave the overall work the potential notoriety of a classic. If it had had nothing to do with him, he would have told Sophia she was every bit as clever as her father. But the shirt on the floor is undeniably his. He'd like to inform Sophia that when he did bring women home, it happened late, and lightly, and he's sure she never witnessed it first hand. He finds it hard to picture her lurking by the stairs. He thinks of the production crew he met in the tech booth half an hour ago moving neatly, capturing each actor's move as it happens.

When he hears the beginning of an orgasm and knows the sex is coming to an end, he lets some saliva back into his mouth.

Shock.

Despite renovations to the exterior lot, theatres in Central London remain impossibly old. Chairs are small. Even with the new rules, where space is left between occupied seats, proximity to others is unavoidable. The great horrified hush around him is tightly strung. It would be so easy to break, and feasibly, to his advantage. How often, he reasons, do groups of middle-class theatre-goers endure watching simulated sex next to strangers? That, he could say in a sensible tone, is not what happened at all. He would not even have to raise his voice too much above normal volume to be heard.

The woman to his right is still grasping her phone and the glove of four sloping bones that make up her knuckles look ready to come out of their skin. For something else to look at, he slants his eyes two seats to his left, where another woman wearing round glasses is sitting. She seems to be having the opposite reaction – she is slouched back; bored. Oddly, the woman with the phone is the older one; from the look of the top of her face, he'd put her in her thirties. Round Glasses looks like she might still be at university, possibly just out of school. She has a buzz cut. Perhaps, he thinks, it's that the younger generation has grown up with an unavoidable stream of sex on their phones: in TV shows, in ads for perfume and cars. She is probably used to it.

Other, terrible, thoughts. Has Sophia heard him come? He listens to the actor do it and decides, evidently not.

More urgent concerns supplant that notion. He has to chew them down. First that Sophia has, however indirectly, thought of him having sex.

It is surprising to him that he cannot receive this idea with more cool. During their holiday, he made sure to write anything radically vulgar without her assistance. And the book they came out with contained very few fucks in the end – mostly, it was almost-adults making innuendo; a lot of anatomical wisecracks and longing. A lot of ships in the night. Part of him had taken it for granted that when she read the finished work, she had skipped over certain passages. The way he recalled it, the part-time nature of their relationship as it existed back then meant they had been distant enough with each other to speak frankly about sex in abstract, or else, to veil it in writer's jargon, but too close for conversation to veer into personal context.

The next problem is that Sophia is aware of the possibility

of his body existing unclothed, and that she has found it to be a problem in the world. He rids himself of the saliva in his mouth.

Sophia is aware he has a dick.

Wrong word. He can feel his tongue prune; ridges on it like an allergic reaction to bad food.

Sophia is aware he has a cock.

No.

A penis.

That settles, somewhat. Who doesn't, after all? But then the next crushing thought. Sophia has written a play in which everyone can see a supposed representation of his penis.

He breathes; moves his knees forward until they touch the seat in front of his. He scans for something meaningless he can look at onstage while he thinks and arrives at the espresso mugs on the kitchen counter. They are plain, and blue.

Sophia has written a play in which everyone can see a supposed representation of his penis, and she has done it to evoke disgust. Possibly he is reading too much into it, but it has turned the woman to his right into a death mask, and the woman to his left cat-like with tedium. Neither option is good. There is enough in him to still feel wounded. If he could walk around the theatre appealing to the audience for help, he would. He's not sure which is the larger slight: that she will continually expose him to a new cohort night after night, or that each show will find his body ugly. And what was she thinking, casting this actor with geometrically cut pubes?

Too quickly, before there's time to stop it, he wonders whether he's supposed to reciprocate. What Sophia has done is undress him with clinical assurance, and perhaps he is supposed to do the same to her play. Someone like him has been conjured; it follows that she might have written herself in, too. If at some point an actress portraying her onstage emerges naked, will he be expected to keep his face level and stern? Should it go like this: here are Sophia's breasts; there is her cunt; here is her body as meaningless event? It is not as though he did not used to, in his own matter-of-fact way, lower her into baths, or unload her from a shit-stained nappy.

But there is a difference, there is. When he finished doing those things, he pressed the soles of her then-tiny feet to his mouth and said, *I love you, you're mine.* None of that care has been given him. In twenty or so years, she might have to wash him while his body degenerates. Will she find him disgusting then? Does it matter?

None of these hold a candle to the remaining fear. Glibly, he had assumed Sophia did not tell him about this play for a long time out of embarrassment; to eliminate the possibility that he might tell her it was bad. So far this is not something he can do in good faith. He'd brought his heart to his seat to watch with, and it turned out there was no need. She was better than him. Now the realisation – perhaps her omission was to spare his feelings, not hers.

(After her father had gone out for the evening, Sophia had weighed up her options. Quiet all around the house. Her mother had told her not to call or text anyone from her phone while she was away; it was too expensive. Her father had not told her whether she could use the landline. She'd had the laptop, but no Wi-Fi, and the proceedings of the day had made the thought of spending more time on the former abhorrent. There had been the brief thought of sneaking out: she might have acted on it – but the thought of going against her father was unprecedented. The novelty of it created a fear response. Relatively speaking, they had spent so little time with one another. In the run-up to their holiday, Sophia had thought of a litany of things living with her father for a month might bring. Greater freedom than her mother allowed; some awkward jokes while they grew used to being around each other. She had not factored in boredom, or a disagreement.

The instinct to make up, as quickly as possible. With no way of knowing when he was due home, she'd found his room and climbed into his bed. She'd reasoned he would wake her up, and that would give her the chance to apologise, and promise to keep helping him with his book.

When water thudded from the tap into the kitchen sink, she'd startled awake. Two voices. For a moment, she'd wondered whether Elena had come back. But the woman speaking called him by his name, not Mister.

Her father had said, *I'll boil some water*—

—and Sophia had come carefully out of his bed. She'd tucked and smoothed the covers. She'd moved slowly on her toes.

In the corridor, sound had amplified: she could hear the racket of plates, and gas on the stove. Someone was putting cups on the table. The crack in her bedroom door had been wide enough to slip past without it opening further.

Reaching her own bed had presented a new conundrum. She could smell her armpits' sweat, the moisture between her breasts and bikini top. Her shorts were still on. If they heard her walk to the bathroom and turn the shower on, they'd know she was awake. She had considered walking to the kitchen or living room on the pretence of a glass of water. But what if they'd been naked? If her father was naked in another room with a strange woman, she did not want to be naked in the same house.

With horror, halfway to her room, Sophia had a fresh thought. Had they gone straight to his bed that night and found her asleep in it? Was that why they hadn't had sex there instead?

More words had filtered through the door. The woman had said, *are you going to love me?* And her father, without pause and in a dispassionate tone she'd never heard him use before, said, No. The sound lodged itself in her mind.)

TWO:
EVERY WOMAN ONSTAGE IS
THE SAME, BUT DIFFERENT

Say you were in the tech booth. No one would speak there. The brightness on the monitors around you would be turned low. Switches on the light board would emit their little clicks when pushed up or down. Whatever sound the room encountered would be fed from microphones onstage into headphones placed around crew members' necks, their heads. You would hear it as a low buzz, a bit of friction fluttering across the room like a moth, crashing softly and stupidly into you with no impact.

From this vantage point, the stage would be visible from a one-way window, cut to 16:9 aspect ratio. The play's crew regularly consult annotated copies of its script and enhance it: carve out the actors' faces in white or blue light, keep the pitch of their hidden mics steady while they move. A digital clock's neon tubes allot the day's hours – currently, 14.45.

You'd see that every so often, members of the audience back row try to be clever. They note changes in the play's atmosphere not evoked by dialogue or expression and turn to the black-tinted glass. They nod, then they face front. They do their best to signal that they are savvy to the made-up nature of what they have paid to watch – they are aware of where the 'magic' happens. Amused, the crew sometimes take bets on how often in a day this happens, barter after-work outdoor pints with tally charts drawn on scrap paper. It's not an exact science. Their attention is too often drawn also to the project's livestream while they work. All of Sophia's words get lifted and reframed by them onto a small screen with an imperceptible lag. This is how you'd see her work become pristine. It makes more sense with close-ups and cutaways. It looks less like two pretend people on a pretend set, projecting to spectators they're ostensibly unaware of. The camera filters out the presence of a stage, an auditorium. It digests the selection of images it's been pointed at and hands them back to you as though they're real.

A line from Sophia's play:
— *You want me to write it with you?*

A line from Sophia's play:
— *Write it for me. I want you to write what I say.*

A line from Sophia's play:
— *What's the difference?*

The other-him, the not-quite-him, and the woman with cropped hair have put their clothes back on and begun writing his book. Sophia's father watches seven years of thought and drafting play out in front of him as a comedy of manners. For the benefit of the audience, his book gets described out loud prior to writing, the way he'd once described it for his daughter before they set about things. It's a neat bit of exposition. So: the book concerns a twenty-something-year-old man with a small ego and a large sex drive — *in other words*, his fictionalised self proclaims, *a well-read virgin*. It is narrated by this protagonist's older self. Most of it is set during the sexual revolution, a time filled not only with the pill and subsequently freed female libido, but also the end of male conscription; the introduction of nuclear threat, of *Protect and Survive*. And, of course, *feminism*. All of this hangs in the air during an Italian holiday the protagonist has been invited to, in the company of his girlfriend and a few of her male friends. The source of the protagonist's misery is one particularly good-looking woman-child with a mythical name and mythical breasts. His onstage self says, *the plot shifts on the questions she provokes. Will our man see her naked? And once he has, will he get to touch her while she's naked?* His partner interrupts, asks, *well, does he care about her? What about his girlfriend?* An exquisitely confused pause emanates from the actor, prolonged by audience laughter. *It's a humiliating experience for everyone involved*, he says.

Conspicuously missing is the point where he explained to Sophia that although the sexual revolution had done away with puritanism and, in turn, enabled the plot they were writing, it had not been replaced with any significant moral framework to allow characters a sense of meaning or satisfaction when they flirted with one another. He had purposefully made the main character utterly impotent. He had made all of his sexual attempts a point of trauma. He remembers telling her, *this is a novel driven by the mistakes of a generation before they realised they were mistakes.* He remembers saying, *this is a novel which anticipates a man's fall from grace for reasons which have conventionally been assigned to women.* He'd brought her in to type up nearly a decade's worth of reflection. It had been a book about girls acting like boys, a rising phenomenon, but by no means novel. He meant it to be cautionary. They were at the start of a new decade, and the rebelliousness he saw brewing in the fairer sex signalled change to come. There was an impatience and agitation at its root. He wanted girls his daughter's age to know that new orders did not happen at the snap of a finger, and demanding that one be taken down without finding a robust replacement was as bad an idea as simply living under threat. Forty years ago, sexual liberation had been supposed to change everything – a free-for-all. That had not been the case; he suspected it would not be now. Having recently entered his fifties, he felt bequeathed of a new wisdom about how things moved. Ageing was painful, but with it there were a few things he could do. Here Sophia is, turning it all into a joke.

His heart thuds away. The woman with small breasts whose orgasm sounds like a steam train is being taught how to take dictation. The people around him think they're watching something funny. Only Round Glasses to his left looks bored. He wants to ask why. Perhaps she's read his books; she might be a fan – she looks like an anarchist with her almost-bald head, like someone who wouldn't care whether it's acceptable or not to like the things he's said. No, he won't be able to tell her everything. She's a stranger. How do you say, *my daughter recreated the longest period of time we've ever spent together and replaced herself with one of my lovers* to a stranger? But he tries it in his head. Round Glasses would react with understandable sympathy and disgust, the way he intended his novels to be read. She might venture a bit of psychoanalysis. She looks like someone who overused all the useless bits of Freud as an undergraduate. She might say, *All girls crave attention from their fathers. Were you particularly absent?* It's a lazy trick; an easy first response. He'd say, the job of a parent is to become unneeded. I was as present as my divorce allowed me to be. I took care of her on weekends until she was old enough to stop visiting.

Time, in his head, is going a lot faster than the action onstage. He makes a catalogue of all the thoughts he has had. He lists them for her, one by one.

True – he had written the final draft of his book by speaking it to another person. Sophia had interrupted his writing almost as often as the woman onstage does to his counterpart. It hadn't been a useful habit. The novel was already fully formed in his head, had seen the benefit of two failed drafts, and his editor's qualified advice. Reciting it to her without notes had been a way to preserve the plot and alter the language. He had not expected her, a few days in, to cut in with suggestions about who should say what, and when, and why. He had not found her interventions, based on how much she liked or disliked a given character, useful.

The actor onstage looks just as frustrated by his com-panion's interruptions as he had been with his daughter's. Of this, he is not proud. Perhaps she is punishing him for a lack of patience.

False – none of the women he'd brought back had stayed at the house for very long. None of his partners, not even Sophia's mother, had ever contributed this directly to his work. Equally false, though sweet of Sophia to think, is the idea that the impulse to write a novel would alight on any occasion in which he'd had the company of a good-looking woman. *That's interesting*, Round Glasses might respond. *You write about women and sexual failure a lot. You write men in a rather feminine way*. He would congratulate her on this observation. I am influenced by women, he would tell her, which is not the same as being helped by them.

True – the atmosphere in the false kitchen is convivial. This other version of himself knows how to mix a cocktail. He serves oranges on a little plate. Around the age of twelve, Sophia had given him a crudely printed mug for Father's Day that read, 'CHEF. TAXI. BANK. DAD.'

That's too personal, Round Glasses says. *It doesn't have anything to do with the play.* Fair enough, he allows, and reframes. True – he had done his best to make sure that, even in the process of writing a novel, everyone had remained fed and watered. At a certain point, when he saw that she had been growing bored, he'd even encouraged Sophia to go off with a friend Elena had found for her.

False – the accusations his fictional lover is throwing at the novel are far more sophisticated than anything his daughter had to say at the time. He watches the actor pronounce the novel's love interests' measurements: bust, waist, hips. *And how big is the main character's dick?* the actress quips. The actor sags. *No one is interested enough in men to care for details like that*, he says.

(Near the end of the second week Sophia and her father had spent in Sicily, Elena had stayed late to wash the floors and launder sheets. Sophia's father had usually been very gracious but insisted he could not work when there was other noise in the house. They'd taken a day off. Elena worked around them. Her father, with seeming ease, smoked and talked. Elena had been preoccupied. Mostly, he had followed her around the house. Sophia heard rivulets of him trailing around. *Perhaps next time you could bring peaches to the house – how do I say peaches in Italian? Pesche, lovely word . . . nice to have a day off . . . rain in England I hear, lots of thunderstorms . . . Venables in prison now where he belongs, foul creature – know who he is? You must be getting paid very well . . . wonderful, every time I come . . . don't suppose you could make that wonderful ricotta of yours . . . sure I can't get you anything, Elena? . . . you old flirt . . . oh, he was here in spring? I haven't seen him very often, the odd phone call, but I think I told you, I introduced him to his wife, years ago . . . returns the favour. I would say I'm lucky, but you know who he's married to . . . peckish, might eat . . .*

Sophia had lain upside down on her bed and dangled a flip-flop off her toe. She had not anticipated Elena speaking

84

suddenly from her door. She'd wanted the sheets; had put the pillows on the floor and gathered all four corners of the bed neatly into a sack. She'd hummed. Sophia watched. Then asked

Elena, where do I go here to have fun?

The turn of her face had seemed to follow on from her nose. Even with so much going on – fringe, make-up, wrinkles, all sharp – the nose made its own impression: clearly boned, and long.

Elena had cleared her throat. Even to Sophia, she addressed her father as *Mister*. She'd said – You ask him if after eight or seven you can go to the beach. Not here, not Canneto. Take the bus or walk. *Spiaggia attrezzata*. Lots of people are there, on holiday, also. They play music outside. She'd mussed her fringe. But you are very young. There are good museums, perhaps?

Elena had smiled at the look on Sophia's face.

You get bored with him.

Sophia had slid her foot out of, then back into, her flip-flop.

No.

Elena had smiled again.

No, Sophia had insisted. I just get bored on my own. He doesn't always want me to help him. I don't know what to do when he's working without me.

After the rest of her conversation with Elena, Sophia had spent dinner working towards asking her father for permission to spend the day out. He got there first.

I gather, he'd said, *that Elena is setting you up with a young man.*

The mushrooms, newly inserted in her mouth, turned. It's her nephew, she told him.

She told me. I want to be very clear, he put his knife and fork down, *I'm putting a lot of trust in you. It's of absolute importance that you leave that boy intact. This is a lovely house and I want to be invited back to it. I'll thank you to avoid any breaking of hearts.* He took his cutlery back up. *What time is your man picking you up?*

I don't know, I suppose Elena has to talk to him first. Don't call him my man.

They chewed.

For two days, Sophia imagined her date. In her head, Elena's nephew looked like the man she'd seen in the gelateria: well-dressed, and tall – only with better English, and a younger face. She tried on sundresses. She tried on blouses and skirts. She practised conversations about her plans for drama school in autumn, and the fact that she was toying with the idea of becoming an actress. She practised flicking her hair behind her shoulder until her wrist adopted the move insouciantly, with grace.

Elena had told her the boy's name was Anto, and that he would take her to see one of the islands nearby as a day-time excursion – there was a volcano there, and it would be unlike anything Sophia had experienced before. He's a good boy, she'd said proudly. Very handsome. Very smart.

At which point Sophia had pivoted to experimenting with nylon skorts and tank tops – tried to choose between ballet flats and plimsolls. Desire waited while she did. Desire won. The plimsolls had been stuffed under her bed. On the night before Anto was due to pick her up, Sophia laid two cotton bras on her bed and considered the advantages of either pink with underwire, or red without. Half an hour into this decision, with the red bra on and the pink held up to her chest, her father had come into her room to call her for dinner. She'd skittered; run behind the door of her wardrobe, and dinner passed in mutually acknowledged silence.

Anto had picked Sophia up outside the house the next day.

She took half a step out, and he said, No. She froze. It took a few seconds for the laughter to reach his face. You will ruin your shoes, he said. You're wearing the wrong clothes – and gestured at the white T-shirt, white one-piece showing through below; her denim shorts.

He had not been tall, or well-dressed. He had dark, curly hair, but there was too much of it in all the wrong places. It massed like fur on his arms and legs; came down gracelessly to the sides of his face. It made an awkward little shadow above his top lip. Still, there was something more assured about his expression than the boys she had gone to school with, and the challenge he issued had provoked in Sophia the desire to be more herself than she had intended. She stood where she was and regarded him coolly.

Then what would you like me to do? She'd asked flatly, and then bristled at the tone with which, *To change would be good*, was delivered. I'm Anto, he'd said then, and smiled. I will wait here for you. He stretched out his arms; seemed to gather the air and space around his person to wait with him. This had been friendly enough. Sophia had relaxed incrementally and nodded.

Try to wear old clothes, he'd advised, whatever you're okay with getting mud on. You have to have strong shoes. And a scarf for your nose and mouth. You'll need water, he'd continued, and sun cream for your skin – a light sweater to stop you from getting burns. Elena said nothing about this?

87

It went better on the boat to Vulcano. She felt self-conscious at first in her father's T-shirt and her own worn plimsolls. But the boat was small, it contained other tourists to watch. Next to the paunch of holiday-goers, the small children with drool-covered chins, Anto held his body loose and laughed easily. Sophia probed him slowly at first, then assuredly to cover any insecurities of her own. He lived in Messina with his parents. He spent a couple of months living with Elena on the islands at this time of year, selling cuttlefish and squid to tourists, to shops. He was not at university. Sophia had said, What do you want to do, then? and he'd looked at her, confused. She'd clarified, in life, which had amused him. He'd said: This, and it seemed to her wise, though she was not sure why. She told him she was going to university in the autumn, and on impulse, at the continued smirk on his face, said, And I'm writing a novel.

She had been glad to see that this engendered respect.

Ah, really? he'd said. I like reading. What is your book about?

It's set in the seventies, she'd recited in her father's voice, and because it's narrated in hindsight by the main character, a man, you get to see the contradiction of how the sexual revolution of his youth wrecks his love life into middle age and beyond. But it's a comedy of manners, really, and I've created some funny characters who drop in and out of the plot to give him bad advice.

Anto had blinked. It sounds interesting, he'd said. I like how it sounds a lot. I wouldn't have expected ... he had gestured at her, and Sophia went slack with triumph.

You don't think I could write a book?

Well, I don't know you, Anto shook his head. Perhaps

88

you could, it's not for me to say. But it's surprising that you can think of the experience of men. When women write books, they're about the opposite. Sad, you know. And always blaming men for everything. You're very impressive.

He had become more attractive to her after that.

Okay, he'd told her. You haven't been to Vulcano before. Sophia shook her head.

Anto laughed. It will smell like rotten eggs, he said. Because of the sulphur. The volcano. You won't be a girl, no? It's only a smell.

Yes, Sophia agreed, and pulled herself up. No need to get dramatic over some bad eggs.

In fact, it had bothered her. From the boat, she saw kneecaps of rock grow closer, red declining into burnt grey, mossed over at the middle with green and bordered by blue sea, blue sky. She willed them to hurry faster towards her. But on the island, she breathed through her mouth; asked, as dispassionately as she could, for his scarf to cover her nose – she had not had one of her own. Her self-consciousness returned when he'd taken out what was, in essence, an old rag. It smelled damp and she could not stop imagining what it looked like on her face.

So, he'd said. We have a few things. Fossa is one of the volcanos in Italy that erupts, but not in a big way for a long time, I think. The beach, obviously. The mud, where we can bathe. It's very good for your health. And, he added, we will stink for days. You will have the memory of this little trip until you manage to wash it off. At this, Sophia had pulled up the rag covering her face. Her nose had wrinkled of its own accord.

He'd said they should hike to the Great Crater first. Swathes of stiff bushes around them, pink with flowers, placated her. There was a chance, she'd hoped, that the hike would take enough time for her to charm him out of the idea of mud baths and into a long lunch. They set off.

Her plimsolls had sunk into the sand at the bottom of the volcano, went in blue and came out ash. Anto had stopped her every so often and told her to drink water: it gave her the chance to take pictures of the green land spotted with toy houses below; the gradual emergence of other islands beyond them: Salina, Filicudi, Panarea. Closest to them was Lipari. It was not a demanding climb. The further they rose, the more Sophia became aware of her father, somewhere on a different cut of rock, working, probably; became aware of herself, rising in circles above him. She imagined this was the sort of view that might be accorded God. She had told Anto so.

You have the name of a goddess, he said. Sophia is . . . how to explain? . . . she is a divine twin of God's son. A female counterpart to Jesus, in a way. Some religions in ancient Rome believed she is something like the mother of this world. So she also has a role in divine creation, very powerful. Perhaps this is why you feel powerful now. Does it happen a lot?

Sophia took a photo of Anto on her phone; turned and framed the Aeolian Islands in her lens. I thought, she'd said wryly, my name meant wisdom.

Yes, that is another aspect of her. If we see each other some more I will tell you how much I think that's true. But so far, it seems it could be right.

Does it? Sophia murmured. Anto had begun to walk again, seeming not to mind the heat that rose with each step up the incline. Yes, he'd said. You are very mature. Your book, for example. It sounds very sensible for someone your age. You're not too much like people your age. Except you're always taking pictures. I'm not a fan of girls who do that. You should enjoy things as they are. Always taking pictures kills the romance.

Sophia put her phone away.

The smell of sulphur at the top of the crater had filled everything. Spots of yellow phosphorescence discoloured the rock – to her it looked like rot. Anto pointed out gas coruscating from fumaroles. The heat they gave off carved itself into bits of their exposed skin: calves, elbows. She had given Anto his cloth back; even he had covered his face now, wrapped his scarf around the bare parts of his neck. She'd covered her own nose and mouth with her cotton cardigan. He stopped her from walking beyond the marked path. She had wanted to point out how strange it was, to have hiked this far up to witness sloping at the peak of all that rock. It had been over 1,600 feet tall and yet its topmost surface depressed into a relatively small hole, speckled neon in some places, burnt dark in others. But the thought of opening her mouth had been unbearable. Anto watched her. With half her face covered, she tried to convey she had had enough, wanted to go down; was tired of walking circles circles circles around the same mound.

On descent, once it had become possible to speak again, Anto told her he felt standing on top of the crater to be very profound. One had a sense of it fulminating beneath their shoes – could be in no doubt that, at any moment, the rock would change its mind and spit them back down to earth. Also, it was the only place you could view the whole archipelago and the northern strait of Sicily, then on as far as Mount Etna. To see a volcano on the horizon from the volcano on which one stood put him always in conflict. For the first few minutes, he felt a sense of wonder and abnormality at the vastness of the situation; felt so very small, standing at the edge of one precipice a hundred times his size to look at another several times that. But after a while, it became normal, was not unlike standing inside a house, looking out of a window at another house, or being in a car, watching other cars pass. He fought to keep that numbness to what was happening away, but, he shrugged, We as people are so stupidly dull. There is never anything to stop our thoughts from destroying the beauty of something we fear may overwhelm us.

These days, Sophia often thinks this sounded like something he'd read in a book and recited to impress himself while he had been with her.)

Skin-on baby potatoes accommodate her mother's fork, shedding pepper and dill along slug trails of oil when moved. Sophia watches her carve them into halves, into quarters, until they settle, newly right angled and exposed. To prevent further tears after Sophia's trip to the bathroom, the tone of the conversation has become carefully formal. Just now, their waiter has withdrawn and her mother has resumed her account.

Between May and June, small tremors had gone through the house. Sophia's father resumed his habit of starting the day in his garden, pacing its perimeter in slippers he wore indoors before shutting himself into his office for an hour to work. He had picked up some commissions from newspapers. I would try to hoover the mulch and soil he dragged in, Sophia's mother says through carrots and pork, and he would come out of the office with a different ailment each day to get me to stop. *I didn't sleep well, I can't take the noise. It's setting off my tinnitus. The hoovering is ruining the copy. I'm finding it difficult to focus. I have a migraine.*

I have always loved, she laughs, the way your father says 'mee-graine'. It's the only thing I've ever wanted to make

93

public about our former marriage. Every time some wide-eyed acolyte gives him a puff piece in *The Times*, I feel like ringing them up and sharing that information. It's so contrary to everything that comes out of his mouth. It's so effete.

Sophia worries over her lemon sole. The ground is too shaky to dispute the choice of word.

As a pacifier in those difficult days, her mother had suggested Sudoku over breakfast every morning. It lasted a week. He had been shit at it and thought he was good – all their puzzles came out wrong. When she lost her temper at him after seven days of mangled work, he told her she had no sense of humour and sulked.

Other, unintended strife they had inflicted on one another. She listened to Radio 3; he didn't like it. He insisted it made him feel as though he were a guest at his own funeral. He smoked indoors; she didn't like it. She insisted it would speed her to an early grave. They had tried setting up an egalitarian household: he would cook, she would clean. I can't say I liked everything he put out, she deadpans. He has a very rich diet. So we took turns doing both.

But the cleaning, instead of creating an accord, had revived their old marital disagreement about degrees of tidiness. One evening, after what she had considered a gentle conversation about microfibre cloths and spills, he had pulled her into the kitchen. He showed her a grease-stained kitchen counter; the sink piled with the remnants of his efforts to make a roast. He said, I've cleaned. Sophia's mother sniffs. I asked him where. Then followed the classically calm conversation that had aided the collapse of their union. Nothing pleased her. He tried his best, and she

made him feel worthless. She'd seen no reason to partici-
pate. There wouldn't have been a divorce to look forward
to this time if she had.

At seventeen, Sophia remembers, the novel she helped
her father write had not been entirely cohesive to her.
There were some parts he wouldn't let her hear. Part of
the confusion was also down to the process of writing
itself – her father didn't always map out plot progression
and intent for her; seldom started the next day's work
where the last had left off. It had been difficult to discern
the meaning of the whole. He had operated on logic she
couldn't understand. Similarly pressing had been the question of allegiance: her father had been a lot less interested
than Sophia in his protagonist's girlfriend, who never said
what Sophia wished she would. She had tried to interject
once at being asked to type the words, *but he did not love
her*; had tried to say – I don't see why he wouldn't, I like
her a lot – and her father had raised a finger to his lips;
made a low shushing noise. For the duration of the book,
the protagonist's girlfriend continued to make reasonable
points in an unreasonable tone. Sophia's father developed
a particular whine whenever he spoke her lines: she would
tell the main character – *you're so unkind* – and with un-
concealed glee he would deliver the sentence in cackled
falsetto.

I understand you, says Sophia. I think we have a similar
problem with him. Her mother picks dill from her teeth
with her tongue. Parts of her cheek and jaw distend while
she hunts. We don't, she says neutrally. The nature of your
problem is abstract. You went on Google and made a list
of all the terrible things he's ever said for money. Possibly,
you feel bad that he once asked you to contribute to that

process before you understood what it meant. My issue is personal.

Isn't mine? Sophia asks. Do you not take it personally when he writes short stories about men falling in love with mannequins, or women growing penises so they can rape their husbands? Does it not feel strange that half his books are about men whose lives are ruined by older women, and the other half feature women getting brutalised? Don't you think that speaks to how he thinks of you, or me?

Her mother finishes fishing, swallows whatever stray food her tongue has caught. It's not to my taste, she allows, but your father writes fiction for a generation less sanitised than yours. He likes to think of himself as a villain in a Western. He used to tell me that he recognised the moral weight of his characters. Shock was a valuable asset in those days: it revealed people to themselves. And really, I suppose I always thought of the men in his novels as a little emasculated. Their lives were always being undone by women. But really, tell me this: outside of the make-believe he makes his money on, have you ever come across a direct quote that says he hates women? In real life, have you ever heard him speak about women less than courteously? Has he ever so much as disciplined you, his daughter? Privately and publicly, he's very happy to be called a feminist.

I don't think he knows what that means anymore, Sophia frowns. Or that his slip-ups are exculpated by age. When I read his books, they're like prolonged rape scenes in films. You say their aim is to expose something wrong, but the amount of glee they hover over pain with says otherwise.

I asked you how *your* father has treated *you* in *real* life. A fork flits towards her from her mother's plate at each emphasised word. Sophia exhales and does not answer. She grips her phone. Online, the CEO of a fast-fashion company popular among millennials has shared a white box filled with text which reads *Over the past few weeks, our retail employees have emailed us to share their lived experiences of transphobic behaviour in our stores . . . This goes against the values which inspire our clothes . . .*

Her mother's series of tuts leave the rest of the post unread. Sophia looks up and waits. She prods the orange peel of her second negroni. Talk, worry, sip. This awkward, stationary cycle. It is not as glamorous as putting on a play was meant to be.

A line from Sophia's play:
— *Would you like a cigarette?*

A line from Sophia's play:
— *I'd love one, yes.*

A line from Sophia's play:
— *Fantastic. You're my kind of woman.*

The first actress has been dispensed with for asking too many questions and replaced with another flat-chested, short-haired brunette. Her entrance happens on the upper set, a shortened, replayed version of the play's introduction. A brief burst of percussion. Then sex. For a moment it's like a record stuck on a loop; confusion saturates the auditorium's red seats – no one knows whether the play has unintentionally restarted, whether the actors have muddled up their script. But this new woman orgasms differently to the first. It sounds like she's sighing. And when she comes down to the kitchen, it looks different too – in the time the set was darkened and attention was drawn elsewhere, the crew has lightly distressed the kitchen cabinets; taken an inch off one of the chairs so that it rocks. Faintly, so lightly it might have almost gone unnoticed, the herbs on the table have wilted. Sophia's father thinks of stagehands in soft-soled shoes, gliding about the kitchen like bandits, taking it ever so slightly apart.

The new actress looks the same as the last one, but she wears a different dress. She listens to the book being explained; the audience listens to the book being explained, again. The actor asks, *would you have a problem writing about matters of sex?* And she, idly, purringly, says, *your sweet talk needs some work.* Then she presents the lead actor with the opposite problem he encountered in the previous act. This new woman leans into the novel's grotesquery with absolute enthusiasm; she hams up its vulgarity to an unworkable extent. As a quick digression from plot, as an allegory to help steady its pace, an attempt to discuss romance vis-à-vis *Jane Eyre* is made. *Not sexy,* she informs the lead actor. He veers quickly into a description of sexual torment. *Not sexy,* is her verdict on this. Sophia's father has to admire the effect. Though he wishes he had nothing to do with it, it's good. It's like the novel Sophia helped him write, but better. He'd spent 400 pages dodging a sex scene on the suspicion that describing people fucking was impossible, and here his daughter is, lacing not one, but two with all the inanity and weight and comedy and power play he always wanted to get across. He'd spent 400 pages anatomising three centuries' worth of the English novel against his generation's attitudes to sex, and here she is, neatly holding just one of his books up against the entirety of her generation's values. He'd spent 400 pages thinking of new ways to describe an erection for a laugh, and here

Sophia is, making a house full of people chortle as the new actress interrupts a speech about the late twentieth century's decline of moral character by slapping a hand over his alter ego's penis.

This thing, this pure kind of meaning she has at work here, is the kind of method he'd always wanted to use in a novel but had never worked out how. It's not the way his mind works. Now, he spends large portions of his days speaking whole sentences again and again until he's caught anything that might make them untrue and changed it. He thinks a published sentence is a duplicate life. He secures each word he uses with utmost care, looks up meaning and origin until it belongs to him, and then sends his work out into the world, where it is still never perfect. Here, not so. Sophia has the benefit of the visual accompanying her work. He sees why she went to drama school now. Who would be a novelist if they knew they could do this? The failure of anything he's written is its inability to translate what he means. The way it looks when light filters through branches of trees; how air smells in the morning, first thing; the feeling in his heart when he looks at people he loves. These are impossible to put down. Yet with the minimum of words required, Sophia has the woman two seats to his left curving her wrist until the sleeve of her cardigan dabs just above her mask. She is crying with laughter. He looks around. She is not the only one. That Sophia, she knows how to pack a punch. She knows that comedy is simply a pattern of misfortune at which the audience is allowed to point and laugh. He thinks,

my girl has them wrapped around her little finger
and swells. He has been weeping, too.

(After her date with Anto, Sophia had smelled of sulphur for days: it kept her mostly indoors. Even having rejected the mud bath, on the boat back she had felt the reek of her body passing off onto other passengers. Her father seemed not to mind, had kept her at the kitchen table regardless and circled around her, dictating. Once, she came to the verge of asking him whether he had noticed anything strange, but his absence of reaction allowed her to forget, occasionally, the taint all over her. At other times, it made things worse. Sophia had wanted both the right to complain and the ability to pretend that nothing had happened.

Elena had taken a more direct approach. For the first two mornings, she'd made a show of holding her nose while laughing gently. He really got you, she said of Anto, and sometimes, Sophia thought, Yes. He did. But she was too well brought up to tell Elena to leave her alone. For a few days, she'd developed a new routine instead. Before Elena's arrival, she went to the beach and bathed in the Tyrrhenian Sea every morning until the skin on her fingers withered inwards. Then she lay on the beach and dried in the sun. When she heard people gathering, when towels were laid close to hers, she ran back to the house, by which point, Elena was gone.

On the fourth day, the smell had more or less worn off. Her father had stopped asking her to help with work. He'd said, Some of it is too grown up for you, cherub, and Sophia, only a handful of weeks away from her eighteenth birthday, had bristled. He was writing a book about teenagers fancying each other on holiday, she argued. She knew more about that than he did. But no, her father insisted. These teenagers were not like her. They weren't in touch with their feelings; they had no consideration. They were vulgar. And hadn't she been bored, recently, with having to help him write?

Sophia had looked her father squarely in the eye. Not wanting to help and being told not to help were two different things. You've told me dirty jokes, she pointed out.

It's not the same, he said. There are better ways you could spend your time. Why don't you see Elena's nephew again? You could learn some Italian, some Roman mythology. You'll have some good material to share with all the people you meet at drama school in the autumn. You want to make yourself interesting, Sophia.

The next night, Anto took her to a resort on the other side of the island. This time she'd known she looked perfect, had olive lipstick and a thin dress on. She'd found scented soap in a nearby pharmacy and showered with it for half an hour. He'd smiled at her on the bus ride over.

How's your book going? he asked.

Sophia floundered, wished she'd checked her father's laptop before leaving and re-read the manuscript's progress. It's good, she nodded, then approximated the look she sometimes saw him wear in the kitchen. Actually, it's tough. Some of the material, by necessity, had to be a little vulgar, she told Anto.

You don't seem like a vulgar person, he smirked. What did she mean by it? Sophia smiled back. I can't discuss it with you, she said. Anto had been sitting by the window seat; he'd turned his face to the glass and laughed. Sophia hadn't been sure whether she liked the sound.

An hour later and settled at the resort's beach club, he'd bought her two drinks and discussed earnestly his philosophy on how to live a simple life. Sleeping, fishing, and good company. She'd quipped it was impressive of him to have worked out how to live when he was barely into his twenties. He'd said, Simple things are always best. For example, all this lipstick you have on. Why? I think natural is good. He'd wiped it off her mouth with his thumb.

When she had finished both cocktails, he led her to the beach by her hand. In the dark, with the static electronic sound of Enrique Iglesias and Pitbull in the air, he moved them behind a low, white wall and pushed her head down.

Mostly, Sophia had found that her jaw ached, that she was bored. She'd wanted to laugh at his little thrusts, and the grabs he made at her hair, and it was that, rather than the smell of saliva and sweat gathering in her nostrils, which brought her back up. She had tried to move his hand under her skirt, but he had withdrawn it boldly with no penitence offered, merely saying, I don't like the way it smells. Still, when they went back to the resort, after two more cocktails, Sophia had found that there was a way not to mind his tongue in her mouth – the large and clumsy insistence of it. She readjusted the straps of her dress during each kiss; sighed when the moment felt appropriate.

In bed the next morning, Sophia spent two hours breathing, obfuscating thought until everything in her was sufficiently distracted not to mind the drop of her wrist and fingers down. When she brought them back up to her nose – no sulphur. Nothing more than something faint, like egg yolks, water, salt, sweat. It smelled of all the things she had been doing. Swimming. Walking. Tasted a little sour. It was nothing very special, after all. He, unwashed, had smelled worse.

She'd met her father at breakfast. He'd peered at her over a volume of George Eliot. Your mother, he grinned, would never have let you stay out as late as you did. Aren't you the lucky one. I hope you used your chance for misbehaviour wisely.

Above the surface of the table Sophia put the muscles in her face on high alert. She smiled placidly over tea and toast.

Did you have a nice time? her father asked, then dispensed an air of silent approval at Sophia's nonchalant, *Nice enough*. And Sophia, without him noticing, had felt part of herself move – she couldn't tell where. Although her stomach untwisted, something like sunstroke had happened to her instead: she sat, slick-palmed, trying not to sway. When she said nothing else, her father looked up, rushed to kneel at her side. Hangover, she told him. He put the back of his hand on her forehead.

We've been here for quite a while now, he said, and we haven't had much quality time together. I'm sorry. I've been writing like mad. Novels are basically maths when you get down to it. I need forty thousand words and I have thirty days . . .

He'd trailed off.

That's a lot, Sophia had said, and wondered whether there was a way to help him better with the job. But he'd sighed. It wasn't too bad. That being said – he'd stood up, resumed his seat – he wanted the two of them to spend a little time out of the house soon. The whole idea of the trip had been to bond. He'd smiled at her. Tomorrow, perhaps. Yes, she'd said. Tomorrow.

That night, he'd gone out without her. Filtered through the walls, Sophia had heard his soft grunts; some strange woman crying *Oh God, Oh God, Oh God*. A different voice every time, but always the shushing sounds that followed – as though her father had been making frequent trips to the cinema, not having sex, and was always upset at having a film he was enjoying spoiled.)

A line from Sophia's play:

  — *It's very rude of you to have brought me here without thinking of dinner.*

A line from Sophia's play:

  — *Later. Please concentrate.*

A line from Sophia's play:

  — *I liked you better when we were having sex.*

Onstage, the second act of Sophia's play moves towards its conclusion on a note of comic reversal. The lead actor has met his match. His second partner has exhausted him with fictional sex. He wants to write smart little vignettes about D.H. Lawrence, about God. He wants to build to the novel's first point of trauma, in which the narrator will drug his girlfriend in an unsuccessful attempt to lose his virginity. But here is his partner, rolling oranges across the kitchen table, watching them drop onto the floor. Here she is, asking, *why don't they just fuck?* – and rising to perch her buttocks on the table's edge. She caresses the lead actor's face with one long, manicured nail. She says, *realistically, you'd rather have a conscious woman to play with, no? Would you like me to show you?*

Sophia's father whispers, *that's not the point*, at the same time the actor does. It's a line he used to give his daughter frequently whenever she queried his book.

This second actress perfectly embodies the accusation thrown at half of the female characters he has written in his life: she's a woman with a cock, she's what his critics like to call a sexpot. And worse, he finds himself reacting in his seat exactly as his fictional double does. He feels sympathy when the other him grabs this woman by the arm and starts to beg, starts to cry, *will you take this seriously?*

I might, she laughs. *How?* the actor says. *What should I do to convince you?* And this actress, so similar in looks to the other, suddenly becomes an entirely new person in Sophia's father's eyes. She stretches a smile over the lower half of her face so slowly and so widely it's a threat.

Fuck me, she says.

Oh, fuck off, the actor weeps. *I already have.*

The lights onstage go dark.

INTERLUDE

Sophia's father has searched his heart and his pockets and the conclusion is a tightly rolled cigarette held lightly in one, sweating palm. He takes it outside. This is how he discovers that Round Glasses from two seats to his left is also a smoker. She tips her chin at him across the road.

I think I know who you are, she says when he approaches. Can't say I'm a fan.

All the patience, all the good will Sophia's father has held in his heart over the course of the past hour drains in the time it takes him to realise that his lighter is in the cloakroom, inside his jacket's pocket. Up until now, he has been very brave. But it is half past three in the afternoon, and even women he's never met before are determined to ruin his life. I had you pegged as anti-institution, he tells her disappointedly.

Oh, I am, she says with one perfectly lifted eyebrow. However she means this, he doesn't get to ask: she has noticed that his cigarette is still unlit. He is touched by the way she cups her palm around its tip despite how gently the breeze hovers around them. She doesn't mind standing close to him, or leaning in to make sure the cigarette has begun to smoke. On closer inspection, she looks his daughter's age. He thinks, I have never been any good at arguing. I have only ever said what's on my mind. So he asks her, without malice, whether she dislikes him because of what they've both watched; does his best to keep his breathing steady in the interval between his question and her answer.

Round Glasses is blunt. She disliked him before, she says. And the play is no great shakes.

They consider the theatre's glass front ahead. Above, gauzy clouds make their modest threats around the perimeter of the sun, continue weakly stirring the air. Do you not like it, Sophia's father ventures, because my daughter wrote it? Is it the association that offends you?

He is horrified by this last question, horrified by the soft pity in her smile. He had meant to speak archly, and now she is looking at him like he's a patient in a sick bed. Would he ever have asked her something like this two hours ago? If someone else had written this play in which some version of him, adapted, reduced, reframed, fucked like a pig and wrote like a dictator – if someone else had put him up there in a two-decade-old shirt he'll never be able to look at again, will probably burn when he gets home (it's such a waste; he never, to his memory, wore it to meet women – he loved it that much) – if someone else had set a whole theatre laughing at him, provoked their open jaws, their mirth, politely veiled behind surgical masks – then, he thinks, there wouldn't be this wan, pathetic feeling inside him, prompting him to ask questions that will leave him utterly debased.

Of course, Round Glasses tells him that she has nothing against him *personally*. She makes this statement sound very noble. She takes issue with his views. As for his daughter, she thinks the play is a waste. The play is smug, obvious white feminism that feeds itself to its audience with a silver spoon. It was social justice for the upper middle class. Its traumas happened in expansive, well-adorned houses. Its bouts of farcical sex on 1,000-thread-count cotton sheets begged to be read as some kind of psychological warfare, or violence. It held up some perfectly common daddy issues and felt itself special for it. I don't mean to offend you, Round Glasses winces, but your daughter's done nothing brave. Her whole conceit makes me cringe. It's actually very common, very BBC. All these white female characters making a show of reclaiming an anglophone novel from a privileged white man. Like that's changing the narrative. Did you know the money this play is running on comes from Arts Council funding for young new artists? Does your daughter even need external funding? I read in one of her interviews that she lives alone in a two-bed in Kentish Town.

Well, she needs a bedroom and an office, Sophia's father says reasonably.

Who pays for that? Round Glasses asks him. He tells her he's sure that's none of her business.

The beginnings of conflict settle, excruciatingly, around them. It's not what he wanted. He feels sorry for her, for her verbal tic of regurgitating fashionable words from the *Guardian* like 'changing the narrative', 'white feminism' and 'privileged white male'. He knows it's the effect of being bombarded with the hurts of strangers every day through a phone. Round Glasses herself is a white woman, wearing Carhartt overalls and pristine Birkenstocks beneath her punky haircut. I'm sorry, he says. She's my daughter. I'm programmed to defend her. Not that I don't have my own issues with the play.

Okay, she smiles. No problem. We can talk about that, too. My point is that the money she's using could have been spent on someone who needs it, with better things to say.

You'll have to help me with that, Sophia's father says. I can't tell whether you think what she's written isn't any good because it doesn't contain your preferred kind of suffering or because, in your eyes, she shouldn't suffer in the first place.

No, it's an okay play, Round Glasses scowls. I didn't mean to say it was objectively bad. It's certainly very well written. I'm sure she has her own very valid personal experiences. But it's style over substance. I have daddy issues, too. You don't see me weeping to all of London about it. There's nothing new or meaningful about what she's done. A thousand other middle-class white women are making work just like hers.

You can't just put on plays because they're written by people who aren't white or middle class. Perhaps other women are writing similarly because what they feel is universal, Sophia's father counters, then is told: Just because something is good doesn't mean it needs to be shown. Historically, people like you and your daughter have had enough money and attention to last you a lifetime. The kind of suffering you describe doesn't hold a candle to what I mean. I can't imagine you'd object to giving less amplified voices a chance to be heard.

This is one of the most irrational forms of critique he's heard, and the ridiculousness of it throws him. He huffs. Sophia has not yet lived half her life. She is only just showing her first, fully realised work after two somewhat middling attempts at local theatres after graduating. She has barely spoken at all; is at the mercy of people like this while she sounds out her early thoughts. He recovers his voice enough to ask, why pay the ticket price for this and not a play by someone you believe in? Wouldn't it be more useful to put money in an 'unprivileged', as you say, person's pocket? Support them? Laud them?

It takes Round Glasses a while to respond. When she does she seems to deflate. I can't – she sounds put out – disagree with something if I haven't seen it with my own eyes.

He likes this bit of honesty from her; appreciates how open the guilt is in her admission. Gently, he shepherds her in its direction, hopes that in doing so they may reach common ground. Say a different kind of woman, one of colour, had written this exact play, he argues. Would you suddenly find it magnificent?

Round Glasses shakes her head. He is missing the point. A woman of colour wouldn't have written the play they were watching. Hasn't Sophia's father been reading the news? In America, across three separate states, there are ongoing investigations into the murders of black civilians shot down by police. One of these was a woman: three plain-clothes officers had forced entry into her home. They had suspected her ex-boyfriend of dealing drugs, they had suspected she might be hiding them for him. They had not believed the multiple statements he'd given that she had no involvement in what he'd been doing. The woman had been shot six times. Her flat had not been searched. In another instance, a trans man had been called – Round Glasses halts for a moment, her mouth seems to twitch involuntarily, she slows down the pace of her outburst, stutters – the 'n' word, and told to stop moving. After he stopped, he was shot. And the case that had garnered the most attention. Surely Sophia's father had seen footage documenting its horror? Of a man, also black, behind an SUV with a police officer's knee pinned on his neck. Of his cries for mercy, for water, for his mother. That he wasn't resisting. That he had been struggling to breathe. That other officers pulled out Mace to keep bystanders attempting to intervene at bay. And what had happened when the man began bleeding from the nose. When he began bleeding from his mouth. When one of the officers checked his pulse, and found none; made no attempt to resuscitate, or give aid.

Why would I watch that? Sophia's father asks, aghast. It sounds as bad as porn. Digitised feasting on the degradation of others. What's your point?

On the pavement opposite, people are still filtering in and out of the theatre at their leisure. Fifteen minutes of the play's interlude remain open to them. Sophia's father watches Round Glasses pick at her chin; watch him with sterile interest. The wobble goes out of her voice. Interesting assessment from a man who writes violent novels filled with murder, sexual violence, and self-loathing characters, she says. I'm trying to tell you that, for some people, times are bad. Not everyone has the luxury of writing Hampstead sex romps via holidays in Italy.

That's facile, Sophia's father frowns. And an impoverishment of the people you claim to care about. It's utterly reductionist. Times have always been bad. The people you're describing have always suffered. Groups beyond them have suffered, too. History has provided us a surfeit of writers to analyse that fact already. Now you say you want more books about these people's sufferance. Why wouldn't you ask for their imagination, or their desire, or their filth, or their wrongs as well? Why wouldn't you believe in the possibility of a non-white Hampstead sex romp via Italian sands?

Because it's not an actualised possibility, Round Glasses seethes. I'd love them to have that freedom. But there are people who have to use what little voice they have teasing out the reality of their suffering until it engenders public sympathy and action, because the government sure as shit won't.

All of your examples are American, Sophia's father points out, because all of your opinions are rephrased junk from strangers who pour their heart out via globalised American media conglomerates on the internet. What about the country you live in? Can you tell me who your Member of Parliament is? Can you name equivalent examples of the cases you described to me just now?

Can you? she laughs. The sound is like a stone being skipped across water; it skurries towards him, dense and small. No, he says confidently once it has drowned. Because I don't pretend to care about things I'm not informed on for the approval of others.

He watches, with triumph, the confidence drain from her face. He is right, and she knows it. But O— he has forgotten the card his own daughter dealt her; too quickly, she remembers how to wield it. It dawns across her face with easy, languid pleasure. Round Glasses flicks the stub of her long-finished cigarette onto the road with one fluid snap of her wrist. She takes out her pouch of tobacco. We've gone off-piste, she says with new-found pleasure. We were talking about your daughter's play. How are you enjoying that?

Self-preservation inspires him to copy her action, to replace his own cigarette. She does not offer to light it this time. It hangs limply in his fingers.

It's interesting, Round Glasses says. She prolongs the process of sliding her own thin cylinder of paper and tobacco back and forth between two fingers and two thumbs. I've been thinking. Is what she's doing so very different to your work as a novelist or a polemicist? You offend people for a living. She's offending you. In a way, she's paid you a great homage. Aren't you proud?

Who have I offended? Sophia's father despairs, aware of his useless right hand holding a useless cigarette. Surely you're smart enough. Read between the lines of anything I've written or said and tell me what there is to be upset about. Comedic flair aside, apply some context instead of raring to be hurt and see who could honestly tell me that I've said something less than kind, neutral, or true in their regard.

Jesus, where to start? She lights her cigarette; exhales its first offering before she counts the list out. Jews. Muslims. Catholics. Christians. Americans. Anyone who died or lost a loved one in 9/11. Gays. Women. Trans women. Immigrants. Jeremy Corbyn. Paris Hilton. The working class. Old people. Old authors. Young authors. Anyone who has dared to pen a less-than-glowing review of one of your books. I expect – she has caught him shaking his head – you'll want to say something to me about free speech.

Nothing of the sort. He wants to say something to her about reading comprehension, about having a sense of humour. She'll have none of it. You don't respect anyone, she says. You don't treat other people with dignity. When he protests this, she holds her cigarette between pursed lips and pulls out her phone. Despite everything, he tries to smile benevolently at her, tries to find something to admire in the hands-free way she continues smoking while she taps at her screen. He watches her lips contort around the cigarette. After a moment she shows the phone to him. She points at a wall of text. Here's you calling one of your critics a prick with a fat backside and a tiny pen. She withdraws the phone again, puffs away until she's found new material. A close-up of Sophia's father's face on BBC 1's *Question Time*; a YouTube clip. She speaks over it while it plays. Here's you saying the average voter has no brains or backbone by way of a golfing analogy. I'm sure it was widely understood. She cuts the video short. A decade-old interview replaces it. Here's you – her face is deadpan – saying you love multiracialism because you've had Polish and Hungarian ex-girlfriends. Here's you, she scrolls down, in the same interview saying iced coffees are for pussies. And further down, that moral order in Europe, whatever that means, would be restored if women committed themselves to being homemakers and having babies. Here's you, she sighs, taking her cigarette out of her mouth, saying the fate of the novel is doomed in the hands of socially confused young authors and that white men are experiencing racism within the publishing industry. She pockets the phone and looks at him expectantly. His tongue, which has been clinging to the roof of his mouth, unsticks itself and lies down in light shock.

You're obsessed, he tells her. Round Glasses shrugs. I'm a freelance culture writer with a journalism degree and access to the internet, she says.

Her cool alerts his. And no compassion, he adds. And no sense.

That might be true, she smiles. I hadn't thought of you as someone whose feelings were so easily hurt. Her cigarette is done. You're late, she says. The interval's over.

THREE:
CORPSING

Pork and lemon sole, barely touched, have been cleared from the table. In the restaurant, Sophia and her mother have justified their continued presence with a large, round plate of carpaccio. It sits between them, in the midst of two other, smaller plates. It glistens redly. Neither woman has much interest in it. They have started to grow tired of the ordinary screams chair legs around them give when pushed out for old guests to exit.

I got so angry with him after I read what you wrote, Sophia's mother says abruptly. She observes the small, empty plate in front of her, traces a finger round its rim. I don't doubt he brought strange women back to where you were staying while you were on holiday with him, underage. It sounds exactly like him. I didn't even need to call you and ask. But then I got angry with you, because you never told me. I had to find out about it through your bloody play after I'd promised you not to tell him anything about it.

Sophia looks up. You didn't, she says. She means this in thanks; she means it as a gesture of hope.

Her mother groans in her chair. I didn't. I wanted to, and couldn't. What was I going to do about it ten years after the fact? I kept you with me for almost eighteen years without him interfering and he still managed to ruin it at the very end. There were days when I was staying with him where I couldn't look at him after reading your play.

In order to read her daughter's work, Sophia's mother had printed the emailed script at a stationery shop close to her ex-husband's home. She had taken it to a café selling artisanal bread and iced buns, and gone through it in one sitting. Paranoia had seized her after reading. To think of it lying on the bedside table in the guest room. To think of Sophia's father finding it there. Unable to imagine anywhere she could hide it safely from his grasp, she had paid £2.90 for her espresso and ditched it in the first bin she saw.

When Sophia's father had greeted her on her return, she'd felt sure something in the pages she'd read had clung to her. He seemed to smell it on her. Late June. They had been bickering already, but after Sophia's mother had read the play, a new distance between them had formed; less courteous than the one before, more remote. He liked to pick at it when bored. *I must be keeping you away from all your lovers*, he'd sulked by the front door one night, after she'd spent the evening out. It had been as though he'd waited for her to come home. The next morning, when he'd seen her hungover, she explained she had been with friends, enjoying sparkling wine and olives in one of their gardens. He had looked pointedly at her, in her unironed cardigan and her house slippers with peeling soles. He had said, *What a sweet little way to spend life's gardening leave.*

And the house had turned. It had never been hers, but after reading Sophia's play, nothing in it gave her comfort. Every object mocked her. Sitting in the kitchen reminded her of what she'd read. Sitting in the living room seemed like an offering of the worst kind. Say she decided to lie on the sofa with a book or a TV show. Her ex-husband would prowl while she did, waiting for a chance to poke at her. Sophia listens with her head bowed. She tries to project respectful silence. From the corner of her eye, she can see her mother's fingers playing with the serving fork, lifting rounds of raw meat one by one on silver prongs before laying each carmine slice back down with new wrinkles, new folds, until the whole platter has been rearranged, disturbed.

She looks desperate. Sophia wishes she would just cry, so that it would be permissible for her to start as well. Instead, her mother launches another grenade. You're so thoughtless, she gasps at her daughter, and gathers speed. Did you ever consider what it would be like for me to read all of that while I was in his house? It was so *strange*, Sophia. I know it's a play, but all those sex scenes; didn't it trouble you, writing that? It's bizarre. Do you want him to love you more? Do you want to be like him? You certainly write like him. Is it because you only saw him twice a week growing up? Because honestly, Sophia, I don't think you have a clue who he is. You've never argued with him. You're doing it now in the safety of your own head.

It's not him, Sophia says. It's a feminist play about men *like* him.

This earns her a reproving glance. It's not him, her mother mimics, and grips her empty glass of wine. It's not him. It's just his book. It's just his shirt you describe in minute detail for the main character to wear the whole way through. I bought that for him. Were you aware of that? I bought it for your father when I married him, before you were born.

The waiter descends upon the carpaccio, sweating on its plate. Is it not to your taste? he asks Sophia and her mother. Would you like a dessert menu instead? He fusses with the table's empty water carafe. To Sophia, he is a saviour; he is the second coming of Christ. She asks him sweetly for more water, another cocktail, for wine to pacify her mother. She tells him to leave the carpaccio, but to come back as soon as he can. Her mother glowers at her after he has left.

It's not very feminist, she says, to write an entire play about your absent father.

Third act. The kitchen is more obviously a wreck. During the interlude, tiles have been removed at random from the wall; the plaster behind them gapes. Dirt has been strewn on the window, on the floor. Another short-haired, flat-chested actress has come – but this time, older. She is the first of these women to somewhat match the lead actor's age. In contrast to them, she looks excessively old, out of place, but it's a trick; it's the crew flooding her with unflattering light; it's what Sophia has done, to make this barely fifty-year-old woman a surprise to the audience. The lead actor helps her down from the upper stage to the lower like a gentleman. It's a new insult. Sophia's father thinks back to the women in their late twenties he has been watching so far: he's never fucked that far beyond his own age group. So this new one, she isn't justice, she's a juxtaposition. His daughter is pitiless, Sophia's father thinks. Not just to him, but to every female character she's wrought. They're devices, they're pointed state-ments, nothing more. People accuse *him* of insensitivity when it comes to gender. Here is this new, *older* woman, tidying up around his alter ego. Like a matron. Like a mum. The lead actor is humming happily at the kitchen table while he explains his work to her for the first time, explains his work to the audience for a third time. Each description has become increasingly grandiose. *Now*, all the missing bits are there. *Now* it's a novel about flawed moral frameworks and generational thought, about sexual trauma, about the fall of man. Now the audience is fully equipped with the spirit of what he meant the book to be about, and what do they do but see it as a discrepancy from the first act, and snicker, and laugh? The new female character busies about in vague assent to everything being said; she opens a kitchen cupboard and exclaims, *Oh, yes, what a lovely book*, extracts coffee granules in a sealed glass jar, offers the lead actor a hot drink. She wipes down counters. How happy he looks with this arrangement. A woman attending to the play's ever more dishevelled kitchen while he writes. Sophia's father looks at the oranges onstage in their bowl – there is an itch in his fingers to climb up there and peel one, to pull the little crescents of flesh apart and set them rocking on a plate.

(Two weeks before their departure her father's patience dropped. He took to walking around the house venting complaints, concerns into the air. Sophia had heard – *past due*; had heard, *not going to finish, fucking deadline,* had heard, *should have done this at home.* His frustrations greyed every room. Sophia felt them in the sofa's upturned cushions whenever he sat to grouse in them, felt them dirtying the kitchen's counter. She remembers suffering. The problem was that he had been so utterly unrepentant. He had made her sit for hours each day without letting her speak; he had made her feel *not special.* She had difficulty raising this fact. It was embarrassing. There had seemed something not very grown up about it, or at least, it was something she had never heard the adults in her life discuss. The revelation that her father somehow anointed her with a daily sense of importance had come to her only through its with-drawal. Each time he left the house to go out at night, she had wanted him to feel terrible. She had wanted him to collapse into one of the chairs next to her at the table and apologise, having searched his heart all night. Instead, he had gone out, and had fun. He used the same tone of voice he made her feel *not special* with to send other women away at night. Then he subjected her to hours of boredom the next morning.

Recusing herself from work became a survival tactic, but the island had run out of charms. Sophia would sit on the beach, alone. She would walk to the gelateria, alone. On a calmer afternoon, she asked her father about the day out he had proposed. Things would seem new to her if he was there. Or perhaps, she asked him, they could take a boat to the mainland, see Messina; she had looked it up the night before. The Museo Regionale had Caravaggios. Not far from there, a mere half an hour's walk, was the Palace of Culture. Come with me, she said.

Her father had been working while she spoke. His typing was slower than hers, was interrupted, on occasion, by his right hand lifting a cigarette. After laying it down, his mouth would remain slightly open, gusts of grey exiting slowly in large clouds. They came out at the start of his re-sponse. Sophia, I really can't, the clouds said. See Anto, take Anto. He's your friend. I'm sure you'll have much more fun. Call him now, use the house phone. And when she didn't, his neck finally turned. Go, her father said. Really, I don't want you to be bored. Do you need the number?

The more she thought about Anto, the less she wanted to see him. Too much shame had accumulated around the memories she had of herself in his presence – flirting, lying, pretending to seem older than she was.

Each dial tone the phone dispensed had been accom-panied by a prayer. Sophia didn't believe in God, but had, as a teenager, made her own private communions whenever she needed to. *I know I only talk to you when things go wrong. That's probably bad*, she'd told God on the first tone, *but if you could just do me this quick favour and make sure he doesn't pick up*, she rushed through the second, *I won't bother Dad again, I'll find a way to do the last two weeks alone, I won't ask for anything else—*

Anto had picked up. You're probably busy, she'd told him.

I don't want to go to Messina, he'd said. The ferries are a robbery. For what? There's nothing in that town. Except my parents. Let's have fun here. Come to my place, it's free. My aunt is working.

She had him meet her at a café instead. Chaste scoops of whipped cream had been dolloped on top of frozen, milky coffee for them. Sophia had prised apart the shining domes of brioche buns accompanying the dessert, dipped pieces into her cup.

It's called granita, Anto said when he brought it over from the counter. Sophia knew. She had been to the café before several times on her own. She had eaten granita alone. It's very good, she'd said. He'd scooped up whipped cream from his glass with his little finger, maintained eye contact while he licked it off. Sophia had pinned her eyes firmly on the café's door to her left until she heard him take up his spoon. Are you not hungry? he'd asked complacently once his dish had been cleared. Pools of melted cream sat under her own glass. We should go, she'd said instead. They'll want to close shop.

This place is open until 2 a.m., Anto told her. But she was right. Why didn't they go to the beach? They might find some of his friends.

Although Anto's friends were his age, none of them spoke English. Eh, they do, a little, Anto had qualified once they'd joined them. We got taught at school. But you don't need it so much here. Don't be English and think badly of them. They don't speak to you because they're shy. They don't want you to hear how terrible they are with your language.

It's not mine, Sophia protested. But why do you speak so well?

I like American films, Anto smiled. You know *Taxi Driver*? Great film. I watched it a lot. When I was your age, I wanted to go to New York as well. Not very accurate about mafia, though. Americans like to say they are Italian. Like *The Godfather*. I'm not so sure. The pasta in that movie looks like shit, you know? Anyway, I wanted to ride in a yellow taxi like De Niro. So I made sure my English was good. I practised on my own.

And did you go? Sophia asked.

No, Anto said. You should, Sophia said. New York is great. It's a bit like London, but there are fewer parks, and everything is a bit more stacked on top of itself. As she'd spoken, she'd seen him become uncomfortable and not known why. He'd said, One day, yes, and changed the topic of conversation abruptly. Had Sophia seen *Taxi Driver*? *The Godfather*? She had not. One of his friends had picked up on the gist of their conversation and set off in rapid Italian. Two hours had passed like this. She fiddled with the laces of her shoes. She piled pebbles on top of one another. She nodded whenever Anto translated fragments of his companions' speech for her, and let him go, lightly, as soon as his attention was pulled away by something she could not understand.

Look, he'd said at last. She had been close to tears.

Sophia followed the direction of Anto's finger. Together, they watched the sky orange over the water, watched it rouge, then purple into dark, until punctures in it opened;

filled with luminescent spots. They enjoyed the reverent hush from the beach around them.

Anto pulled her up from the ground. Life had broken out, restarted in the new dark: his friends were laughing again, lighting cigarettes. Elsewhere, other groups of young people were arriving. Despite the boredom she had felt, Sophia wanted to stay. Here, finally, was the environment she had imagined when she'd said yes to her father's trip – if she could only convince Anto to translate more for her, to teach her how to say the things she wanted to say. She could make more of an effort now. Someone else had come with a box of small beers; they were being opened. But he'd had enough. He wanted to find a bar. He gripped her palm and said goodbye to his friends below. Come, he said. They'd left.

Tomorrow, there's a festival, he told her while they walked. It lasts four days. The Festival of Saint Bartholomew the Apostle. He's the patron saint of Lipari, he protects these islands. The big day of celebration is on Tuesday: the whole island comes out to carry a statue to the beach. That's not so much fun. But if you follow the crowd with friends, stop for a few drinks, maybe get a little drunk, at the end, there are fireworks. Everyone will be in a good mood. Will you join us?

Sophia had stopped where she was. That's my father, she'd said. There he'd been, in a short-sleeved, purple paisley shirt, striding purposefully before them. An apparition. Patches of sweat under his armpits. It had been impossible to know where he had appeared from, how long he had been there, but he had not seemed aware of them. Anto had examined the back of his head, tugged Sophia's arm until she followed. They'd walked behind him. Anto kept saying, *that's not how my aunt described his looks*, and Sophia had shushed him each time – whatever Elena had said, she preferred not to know. Enough people surrounded them for cover, and balconies bore down from overhead dispensing their distractions. Periodically, Sophia's father had looked up, and never around.

I know where he's going, Anto told Sophia. This is very funny. I was going to take you there also. Should we go somewhere else or should we say hello?

I don't want to say hello, Sophia whispered; repeated the statement guardedly into Anto's ear. He looked down at her. His expression had been oddly pleased. Sophia had glimpsed, for the first time in his company, his resemblance to his aunt, the ridge in his nose.

Let's spy on him, Anto laughed. Without saying hello. What does he get up to without you? Let's find out.)

Wound around the bowl of a refilled wine glass is her mother's hand. She had been all set to leave in July, she tells Sophia. She had had enough. Neglect had seeped through the pockets of her own home, and the upkeep of her ex-husband's had become intolerable. That, she tells Sophia, I did like. The kitchen falling apart in your play. I could see it happening in my house, and in his, once I had decided to stop acting as his maid. He told me he'd had one, as well. He paid her all through lockdown in the hope that she'd come visit him. I never saw her. She owes me a cut of money, though.

Picpoul sloshes towards Sophia, threatens the carpaccio and the tablecloth each time her mother thrusts the glass forward to emphasise her point.

He didn't clean. He didn't do dishes. You keep saying the same things about him, Sophia says.

Because, her mother cries, he kept *doing* them.

She had taken out her suitcase. She had folded her clothes into its corners.

But you didn't go, Sophia says.

Obviously not. Sophia's mother reclaims her dignity with

a slice of raw meat. The hole it leaves in the arrangement is bleached; stark. She makes a show of thinking while she chews.

With purpose, having packed, she'd descended to meet Sophia's father, just back from his evening constitutional. Instead: some small talk. Pleasantries exchanged across the living room, with him on the sofa and her at the door. He'd spent his walk on the phone with an old classmate, had thought of inviting her for dinner and hoped Sophia's mother would be there. Hadn't they used to throw good dinner parties when they'd first moved in together? She could invite some friends of her own. Wouldn't it be the perfect excuse to restock on booze? She could help him choose. Her taste had always been better than his. In fact – he had risen from the couch – he had been thinking of a drink and would be glad of the company.

Better to leave on good terms, Sophia's mother had reasoned.

Port, poured into small glasses over the island in the kitchen while she perched on one of its stools. It had felt like a date.

When she left, he'd said to her then, he'd only borne her a reasonable amount of ill will. And hadn't the past few weeks proved that she remained the patron saint of fairness – that something in her, still, wanted to take care of him? It perturbed him in his late thirties that he would never be able to write a book about her. Their marriage had been his mistake. But gradually, he had come to the conclusion that irreconcilable differences in their case meant that he continued going out when she started staying home; that he forgot to ask about how her day had gone in the miasma of a morning hangover. He remembered one night, after putting Sophia down for bed, how she had put him outside the front door like a dog and told him plainly she had no intention of living in a house with two children. He could leave and carry on however he liked, or he could come back indoors and behave like an adult. He remembered, to his shame, chain smoking on the front step for half an hour before he came in. He wasn't proud of that. It was as clear to him then as it was now that the qualities she had fallen in love with him for, the loudness and blitheness, the odd mix of sentimentalism tempered with sharp verbal wit, were things she expected to mature in him. He had never seen it this way and neglected to tell her from the off. These were core traits he expected to maintain until he died.

But, ah – he had laughed at the expression on her face – he still remembered the first time he saw her: how she had been trying to hail a cab, and on the turn of a second, he'd run to thrust himself into the one that stopped before she got away. The tail of a red coat had been disappearing into the door. He'd pretended to argue with her about whose taxi it was until the driver informed them that it was, in fact, the lady's joint and unless she agreed to share it with him, he would have to leave. Before her mouth could open he'd told her to look into his eyes – did she remember that? Of course, she'd declined – but, as he put it, if she never looked into anyone's eyes, how would she ever fall in love?

It was an awful line, designed to exasperate her into telling the cabbie to drive on, and it worked. He had exasperated her into love. Neither of them could have been surprised that the process would one day invert itself. But there she was, drinking port with him, eating breakfast with him, talking to him every day with her low voice and the abundant gaps of space she left between words while thinking.

He had shocked her, Sophia's mother tells her daughter. He had shocked her into staying, into wanting to hear whether he would say something more.

A line from Sophia's play:
— *Sit down now.*

A line from Sophia's play:
— *Yes, yes. Just as soon as I've swept the floor.*

A line from Sophia's play:
— *Sit down. Now.*

The older actress keeps cleaning; she is so utterly un-interested in the lead actor's book. She dusts the tops of the kitchen cupboards; she rearranges the eggs in their bowl. She pinches the lead actor's cheek until it blots pretty and pink. It's like a pantomime. She goes up, he sits her down, and the audience laughs. *You're a messy boy,* she tells him.

Sophia's father sneers in his velvet chair. When he comes out of this theatre, what will he be like in the world? Will he still have a daughter? Will strangers speak about him as a dirty old man with no compassion for people, who shouts like a tyrant when he writes? His body is begging him to leave his seat. He wasted the interval with Round Glasses and now he needs a piss. The play ends in less than an hour. He doesn't know whether he remembers where the toilets are. The liquid in his bladder has rattled him enough to think of finding Round Glasses, wherever she might be in the world, and tell her that her opinions are shit. Also, that she has caused him discomfort.

Floating, disparate thoughts. Are the eggs on the table real? Is it someone's job to go to the Tesco around the corner on the Strand every day and rebuy bunches of fresh herbs? He hasn't checked in on the woman to his right in a while. When he does, he is surprised to find she is glaring at his knee: it is jumping up and down with the effort of not getting up for the toilet. Sophia's father whispers, sorry, and to his surprise it feels good to have spoken, to have broken through the forced silence in the air. People behind him push air through their lips to quiet him. He begins to understand the appeal of fiddling with a phone for the first half, the way the woman to the right often does. Speaking out loud has been an insertion of sorts; it makes the play more his own. Other people have noticed it, too. He wonders what else he can do while the actors talk. He wonders what he's done to have become so abysmally misunderstood by the most important person in his life. He does not know how to fix it. Raising Sophia part-time was a constant conundrum between being her father and her friend – of creating a different closeness than the one she had with her mother so that no chance of comparison could arise between them. He had wanted to be her father, yes, but also a confidant for any difficulties she had during the days she spent without him. Hundreds of times, there had been the anxiety of trying not to get things wrong, and then getting them wrong anyway. Her first period, bad Christmas presents, boring weekends. Saying the wrong thing when she was upset, offering objective advice first before he delivered a hug. That the expectations he had of life as he came into adulthood were so different from hers, that they lived in utterly different versions of modernity, was sometimes hard. And still, he'd thought, she loved him anyway. Was it not the case that she had accepted or at least rolled her eyes at jokes that grew ever more contentious across the time he made them? When they disagreed about pronouns, about politicians – none of this mattered. He closes his eyes to the actress onstage, washing her pale, busy hands.

(Detective work had suited Anto. He'd walked ahead, maintained a considered distance between Sophia and her father, craning his neck at one and throwing mischievous looks over his shoulder to the other. At the foot of a thin passage brokered by tall houses he had put his arm out. He felt confident, he told Sophia, that her father would enter a wine bar on the left side of where they stood. They had to let him go in first. Then, Anto conspired, they could take one of the tables outside, whichever was closest to the door. It would be impossible to follow him inside, he told Sophia, because the bar was very small; he would see them instantly. But by dragging the table closer to the open doorway, Anto felt sure he could keep an eye on what was going on while Sophia remained hidden.

Sophia committed herself to being unseen. She let Anto place his hands on her shoulders and steer her where he wanted; she tucked her elbows into her sides when he placed her in her chair. She listened to his objections that she could not order her preferred choice of cocktail, lest that tip her father off to her presence there. What's something you would never drink? Anto bounced above her, bounced over the table in ecstasy, like a child at their own birthday party, like the worst waiter in the world. Gin, Sophia said. She watched him pass through the door to place their orders.

Boring so far, Anto said on his return. He's reading a book. Drinking something.

On the table, a slender triangle of brined juniper, two floating olives on a skewer. Sophia plucked Anto's daquiri from his hand when he sat down. What kind of drink? she asked. What kind of book? Anto had stared at his empty palm. No, he said to it. I didn't look. I don't know.

Antipasti were brought. There had been no gate or barrier to distinguish the bar's outdoor area from the street in general. People brushed past; Sophia watched them. The passage they sat in had been so narrow she had smelled their various odours: powder, cologne, sweat under the arms. Elegant women with curled hair strode by; men in salmon-pink shorts attended them. Older couples locked peacefully arm in arm coloured their surroundings, beautifully burnished by the lambent glow of iron lamps hung from nearby walls. Sophia's stomach, furnished with ciabatta and provolone, leapt happily at each stranger. She recounted what she liked about them to Anto, who nodded or shrugged; explained how common or uncommon it was to see whatever she noticed around her. Periodically, he would recline until his body stretched into a perfect diagonal line, shirt rising over his stomach. Sophia watched the thatch of black hair on his stomach emerge, watched his head loll with practised laziness towards the door. Still reading, would be the report, until, one empty daquiri glass later, it wasn't.

Oh, Anto said, back extended in his chair. He's talking to someone. Does he have friends here?

143

Sophia had gripped her empty cocktail, hoovered the remaining drops of melted ice and rum through its straw so that air bubbled around the glass in dull, continuous pops. His friends aren't here, she told Anto. Your aunt knows them. They've lent us their house for the summer. Have you met them?

Anto said he hadn't. He had never been to the house his aunt sometimes took care of. She had described it to him once. He knew it was very big.

The martini glass sat before him, still full. They needed more to drink, he'd decided. He would order more cocktails and get a closer look at her father's companion.

Sophia had counted out the seconds of his absence. She had breathed in through her nose and out through her mouth. Time contracted to the wild asters standing decoratively to attention in the middle of their small table. When Anto returned, he held an espresso martini in one hand and a gin martini in the other.

She's got short brown hair like a boy, he said. Very pretty, but not my type. English men have a problem with curves, no? I think she's also a tourist. She doesn't look Sicilian.

Lines formed between his eyes while Sophia switched the placement of their cocktails. Please – he'd spoken firmly – this is becoming rude.

I didn't want gin, Sophia pointed out. I told you I don't really drink it. If you don't want it either, go back inside for something else and tell me what they're talking about.

He'd said something in Italian; placed a slice of salami under his tongue before making his way back into the bar. This time, Sophia had lifted herself carefully from her chair; eased herself into his, opposite. As though loud music hadn't been blaring from the building's entryway.

As though she were at home, late at night, trying not to let her father know she was awake. She stretched herself out as Anto had done, arms above her head. She dropped her head in the direction of the door. Sooty air. Huddles of clothing. She searched for purple paisley fabric. She yawned to prolong her apparent need to continue stretching.

Not on the first yawn, nor the second, she found it and whipped her body back. Her father's arm across someone's chair. Her father's lips at someone's neck.

Yes, very friendly, Anto had confirmed, once a vodka and coke had been placed into his tightly clenched fingers. I'm not sure I fully understood, but he's telling her something about Nabokov. Over the rim of his glass, he had studied Sophia's face. Where's your mother? he asked. You don't talk about her. Do you have one?

Everyone has a mother, Sophia said. Anto shook his head. Not everyone. Some people were unlucky.

She's in England, came the reply. She's not here. And Anto had blinked, suddenly inconsolable. He looked to the door of the bar, then to Sophia; to the door of the bar, then back. On her own, he said. In England without you both. You both came without her. I would never do that to my mama. Is she okay? Does she have people, while you're away? Don't you miss her?

You're away from your mother now, Sophia said irritably. But no, that was different. Anto's father was there to take care of her. Anto called home once a day to make sure all was well. My parents are divorced, Sophia had said, and Anto made a soft *ahhh* sound. Now he looked to the open door of the bar with newly acquired knowledge: it had spread on his face as a smile. Divorced, he said. Of course.)

Sophia takes an untouched glass and the carafe; she pushes water across the table. Hiccups are pulling her mother's sentences ever so slightly out of tune. She is telling her daughter something urgently – like so:

It had taken another week for Sophia's father to broach the subject of their long-finished marriage. *Hiccup*. But when he did, it was confessional. You picked up after me too much, I know. *Hiccup*. That was what he had said. Partly in the spirit of regret. But also because he regretted that he had never found a way to make her relax. She was forever tidying. *Hiccup*. Picking up his shoes, Sophia's toys. Washing linen, soup bowls. And the fact that she had done it all so uncomplainingly had made it worse. *Hiccup*. He'd told Sophia's mother he'd tried to tidy, too, but his efforts were no use to her. *Hiccup*. At a certain point, it seemed more use to get her to remember how to have fun. But she never wanted to. *Hiccup*. It made him incredibly sad. She'd been against hiring a nanny, so could not go to parties. She had not had the energy for listening to music, reading books. *Hiccup*. At the time, it had been isolating for him. She had paid so much attention to their daughter. She had none left to spare for him.

146

For the love of God, Sophia murmurs. Have some water. She waits while her mother holds her breath.

Sounds appalling, of course, is the first thing her mother says on exhale. The hiccups have gone. Yes, it had been just as insufferable to listen to as it was to experience. But then—

He had told her his regrets. That when he'd bought his new house after they separated, he had begun to distinguish what was around him through empty space, rather than filled.

To counter this, he had thrown parties. He had welcomed newcomers' cigarette smoke and abandoned cocktail glasses as interior décor. The cavernousness of the house became something to be occupied. But during the day, the sudden lack of his wife and child made sound echo in ways it hadn't before. He had thought about getting a dog and found himself unwilling to face the idea of taking the thing out for a walk every day. He had thought about a cat or a budgie, but neither option suited his self-image. He installed, instead, an aquarium with the intent of filling it with as many rare curiosities as he could – made lists and sometimes even managed to procure petrochromis, golden gars, flowerhorn cichlids. Dappled blue light got thrown onto the living room rug. The inside of the tank was an expensive rainbow to meditate on over his morning coffee. It had required little effort.

Sophia's mother shakes her head briefly, resumes. A month after acquiring it, he'd told her, he'd thrown a house party. The fish were the centrepiece. Guests had clustered politely around it for the first few minutes of the evening, stopping every so often to amuse themselves with his new hobby. They gave the fish names, genders, funny voices, entire life stories. When the newness of it wore off, the tank went ignored. Everyone got on with their drinks and gossip until two of his friends had a falling out. Sophia's father had been unable to remember what it concerned. The memory had been hazy in his mind, both because he'd had a lot of whisky, but also because the disagreement culminated in one of the injured parties being put through the aquarium.

Glass went everywhere. Pebbles and coral fell like marbles over the floor. He'd remembered everyone kneeling, not towards the men, cut and panting on the floor, but towards the fish: scrabbling and grabbing handfuls of scaly colour; throwing them into their glasses of wine, their beer. The injuries when people grabbed broken glass by mistake. Some guests had even remembered the names they had given each animal and ushered them into flutes or tumblers as though they were coaxing a child to bed on a school night.

When there were no fish left on the floor, two first aid kits were found. The next morning, Sophia's father had gone downstairs. Blood on the rug. Dead fish floating in claret and lager and Martini Rosso. Alcohol poisoning rather than suffocation. He'd wondered whether they had at least got drunk before they passed. The emptiness of the house was a tolerable alternative after that.

Fuck, Sophia breathes. And then what?

And then—

Her mother starts to laugh. The sound is terrible. It disrupts the room at large; it makes people look over at them in disapproval while, between cackles, her mother pushes words out.

And then he told me, after all those months imprisoned together, how much he still missed having me around.

But how quickly the statement had been qualified. Perhaps that had not been it. Perhaps he missed being married. No— not married, that wasn't it, really. He had told her: evidently, he still got on her nerves. She still got on his. But wasn't it true that he still couldn't find a woman to hold a candle to her?

All the while, the lead actor has been having a tantrum onstage. He has been chastising the new woman he has brought home for not being helpful enough in the way he wants. She doesn't listen when he talks; she does whatever she wants. He is trying his best to pack her off neatly into the play's pretend night. Sophia's father watches her; she has acquired an apron. She sounds just like his ex-wife. She is complaining about mess and his alter ego's bad habits when it comes to missing dinner. She is standing over the set's stove with her back to the audience, guiding chopped garlic and onions down a cutting board with her knife. They slide onto a pan, noiseless. No smell comes off them. Even the stove is make-believe, a fake. Sophia's father snorts, makes no attempt to cover the sound. Pain has settled between his hips. He might wet himself; he might scream. He might climb onstage and clean the kitchen himself to get the actress to shut up.

(Having gone into the bar for another cocktail, Anto shot out; pulled Sophia's arm with a gleeful whoop. Sophia had heard, *he's paying, he's coming, they're coming now. Run — RUN* — and she had. She had stumbled around the corner of their table, unhooking her bag from the back of her chair. His legs were longer than hers, took the length of the passageway they had come down in lax, easy bounds.

They had not stopped running at its end. Sophia saw him slow to grasp her hand; felt the sharp pull he exerted on it in her shoulder. Past the port, then up, towards another row of shops. Sharpness in her chest at each road's incline. The rub of dirty cotton plimsolls at the base and sides of each foot. Anto kept them running until she couldn't form a coherent thought. He pushed them past strangers. When they stopped, adrenaline dilated and rebirthed itself as panic in Sophia's legs. To the left of a small grocery shop, she pressed her cheek onto the wall. She gasped into ridged plaster. Anto's palm fell from hers.

My aunt's place, he'd panted. I'll get you water. He walked towards her. A key extracted from his pocket latched smoothly into a door she hadn't noticed next to the shop. Can you walk? he said. I'll lift you.

Her legs had trembled loosely in the air; his arms had trembled around them. Past a flight of stairs, Anto set Sophia down and retrieved another key for the door at the top of them.

It had not been what Sophia expected. The house looked nothing like her father's friends'. Scalpels of harsh light came down from rectangular bulbs affixed to the ceiling. A kitchenette opened out into a living room. Garden furniture, plastic and white, shone at its edge. A velvet red sofa, clean, but chewed, sagged in the corner. She'd collapsed on it, thanked Anto while he held a pint glass under the sink's tap.

No patterns, or tastefully mixed colours. No blankets, or rugs. In a glass cabinet, some photos of Elena with strangers: one might have been Anto's mother. There was an image of Anto himself, wearing a robe and a wreath in his hair. Beside it, ornately framed, an image of the Madonna. Sophia noticed a crucifix above the apartment's door.

Elena's plastic table held a knitted vase of felted flowers; Anto hid them underneath the sofa when he brought Sophia her water. Did you make those? she'd asked. No. He spread his legs into a large V. His little sister had, years ago. He didn't like them very much. Drink, he implored.

Your father is funny, she'd heard with her face buried in the pint glass. He was looking at that woman like this—

When she'd lifted her face, Sophia had seen Anto's head tilted onto his shoulder, his eyes half closed, his mouth slightly open.

Disgust compelled her. I have to go to the toilet, she'd said.

The washroom had been small; the comfort it provided

had been small. Sophia had wrinkled her nose at the furred, circular rug with a hole in its middle gripping the toilet's base. Pink soap, already damp, melted at the top of the sink, dyeing rivulets of water around it. She held it between two fingers and felt her nails pierce through the sides. Softened clumps adhered to her fingers. It was all too much. She washed her hands without it, washed her hands again while she thought of what to do. No answer came. Back in the living room, Anto had spread his legs still further on the couch. We can go to my room, he said.

Here is good, Sophia replied. Seconds passed. They made her standing away from him seem ridiculous. There was no choice but to return to where he was. On her descent, Anto extended an arm behind her, hugged one stiff shoulder until she moved towards his chest.

I feel better, she prompted.

He smiled at her. That's good.

The arm pinched harder. Elena's face sparkled from the cabinets.

Where does your aunt sleep? Sophia asked him.

On this sofa. He had been reaching for her chin with his thumb. I tell her not to, but she wants me to have the bed. What can I do? You have to respect your elders.

And then the kiss – nothing new: she had felt what it was like before, knew what Anto liked to do with his tongue. Disliking it more than she had the first time was not the only issue. Pressed into the couch was the ghost of Elena's sleeping form. The threat that she might at any moment walk through the front door gathered itself in Sophia's heart. The images of her holding children, hugging other people, were all around them, making worse the sparseness of her home, its pale walls; making worse the idea of her mopping and cleaning this place the way she did the house Sophia's father had borrowed; making worse the idea of her eating in it the way she never did in the house Sophia's father had borrowed, opening the tinned tomatoes stacked on the kitchen counter, drinking from the glass Sophia had now drunk from, too.

Anto stopped kissing her. His eyes had been half-closed. His mouth had been slightly open. Sophia had pulled at the skirt of her dress, looked around the flat.

I'm not very comfortable, she said. Anto's eyes followed wherever hers fell, observed whatever surface she looked at. Then he looked at her. She had not been able to tell whether he was angry or hurt. Both expressions might have looked the same. Sophia bit her lip and delivered her coup de grâce—

I'm on my period, she lied. I don't have another tampon.

It worked like clockwork. He'd withdrawn.

Please, don't look for any. She had jerked upwards when he made to move. I'm sure your aunt doesn't have them.

It wasn't my intent, Anto said levelly. There's the shop downstairs if you need to find them.

He listened to her rushed apologies. He sat alone on the sofa when she went out the door.

And the next morning, as though Sophia had willed them into being: cramps. Clots on the toilet's clean, white bowl. After cleaning herself, she had been reading at the kitchen table while her father worked, ignoring the quilted plastic, tacky on one side, clinging limply to her knickers when—

Eleven o'clock.

Anto had rung the doorbell holding flowers. Anto had rung the doorbell holding wine.)

But would you believe it, *he started showing me love.*

Sophia's mother laughs harder than before. After the conversation about their marriage, candles in silver holders had appeared on the kitchen's island, dropping wax softly onto marble after dark. Sprigs of lavender began hiding among books on the shelves. 'Blue in Green' played on speakers around the house.

Her mother goads air out of her mouth as though it is no longer precious to her. It moves without flinching around the restaurant.

Would Sophia believe, she rasped, that it was as though her father had felt they'd resolved the wreckage of their marriage to their mutual satisfaction? All the women he'd openly stared at – gone. All the accusations he made in her direction, erased. With a little Bordeaux, and the pile of expensive creams she found one day in the guest bathroom, he had expected her,

(that phrase shrieked a pitch higher)

to forget how much time she had wasted in her life because he was inept at thawing breast milk at least two hours before it was needed; because it had been necessary to lock himself in a room and make believe. That he had never given this time back to her in the form of laundry, or trips to the shop for dinner, or lunch. That when they divorced, only seeing Sophia for two days a week had been *his* request, not hers.

Madame. Their server has appeared, his hands locked firmly before his stomach. I must ask you to be considerate of our clientele. We would appreciate if the volume of the fun you're having could be restricted to your table.

Sophia's mother blinks lazily at him. Can I have some more wine? she asks.

I must ask you, the waiter repeats, to lower your voice.

Yes, Sophia's mother snaps. I heard you the first time. *I must ask you* to bring another glass of Picpoul on your next run.

Please, Sophia inserts. She looks miserably at their server's receding form. American businessmen in suits, children with soup stains on their shirts, staff on their break from the theatre, senior citizens, young women with French-tipped nails and lip filler, have all turned to witness the spectacle. Her mother chuckles into her wine glass.

I *am* having fun at last, she says.

You're drunk. Sophia strains forward. I need you not to be drunk. I wanted you here to help me with how awful it feels to wait while he watches my play. Please.

I'm tipsy, not drunk, her mother tells her with a bluntness that approaches relish. I'm having a nice time.

Recently, she continues, ignoring the desperation on her daughter's face, she had found herself thinking of her own mother, who had divorced even younger than she had. She'd bought a patch of land when she'd finished raising Sophia's mother; lived out the rest of her life three

156

miles away from a remote little town. She'd grown potatoes, strawberries, mint, in her garden. She'd scattered
corn for hens in the morning and wrung their necks at
night. She had a cow. She had milk, and butter. She never
asked a thing of anyone. She'd never asked for love after
her marriage.

Granny was bitter, Sophia whispers. You didn't like her.

Granny was a genius, her mother smiles, and laughs, and
laughs.

The audience laughs, too. Someone new has climaxed: she's blonde this time, with a fresh face and slender ankles. The lead actor is sheepishly rubbing his stomach while she gets dressed. They're in the kitchen, and when she finishes, she sits herself expectantly at one end of the table. *I'm sorry*, he says. *This is a slightly novel experience for me.* Ha, goes the audience, ha. Even the lead actor corpses for a moment.

The kitchen has been bombed beyond recognition: the table slopes on three legs, the glass in the window is fractured. It's unclear how the crew could have managed this, even during the play's customary five minutes of loud sex, with the lights on the lower stage lowered. They have trashed the recreation of a place Sophia's father loves very much. He thinks he will die in his seat.

When the matinee ends, will he have a daughter? He is supposed to meet her in the theatre's rooftop restaurant and bar.

The lead actor is toying with his new plaything's blonde hair, he is explaining the end of his book. He is muddling the timeline of what Sophia's father originally wrote.

Wrong, Sophia's father mutters dully. Beneath their masks,

the audience is smirking – he feels sure of it; when he twists around (but his bladder is so full, and it hurts, it hurts) all the cotton on their faces is stretching out of place – and the cow to his right is shushing him; he could say something back,

(Sophia had willed Anto away from the door when it opened, grabbed the flowers and the alcohol, and thanked him very much. It's not a good time, she said. You have to go. But Anto had laughed: *my Eengleesh very bad. You want me to come through?* He'd placed a polished shoe onto the threshold. Sophia kicked it with her bare foot. Not now, she said, but it had been no use: her father had come to see what the fuss was about, to invite Anto in – he had been curious about this young man, of whom Elena spoke so highly. There was nothing to be done. Anto had been seated in the living room. That morning, he had worn a stiff, long-sleeved shirt. He had combed his hair down. The wine is for you, Anto nodded at Sophia's father, and the flowers are for your daughter.

How beautiful, Sophia's father said dryly; left both items in his daughter's hands. Anto preened beside the sofa's hand-embroidered cushions.

The uncertainty of the previous night. She had not left Elena's flat very late, it turned out. But if Anto had seen her father paying the tab at the wine bar with his companion, how would she be able to go home without interrupting them both? The image of lidded eyes and gaping mouths soured in her stomach. Sophia had decided to go back to the wine bar and wait as long as she could.

Her father had been there, red-faced in his purple shirt, still stroking the brunette woman's arm, her thigh.

And her father was there now, in the kitchen, uncorking Anto's wine. Sophia had thought of last night's bus home; the two hours of peace in which she had been able to cry, she hadn't even been sure what over – but her legs had hurt, and her mouth felt dirty, and when, at half past one in the morning, the latch in the door had clicked open, more tears fell. It had been impossible to sleep through it that time.

Do I spare Anto, her father asked; nudged an elbow into Sophia's T-shirt. Or not? Should we have some fun? I must say though – then sniffing the extracted cork – he's got good taste in booze,)

And Sophia is still listening to the crowing that intrudes on the good standing of the restaurant – her mother is incandescent; Sophia has never seen her face look like it does now, Sophia has never heard her voice sound like it does now, as she laughs:

—and Sophia's father, stuck in his chair, really thinks he
should say something, he
   really thinks
   he should
   say
   something,

(And the questions he had asked Anto had been questions he'd never asked her: serious enquiries, about ambition, about life – Sophia had watched them huddling on the sofa, conspiring together

Sophia had watched them trade opinions on city living
– not that Anto had ever lived in a city –
on Italo Calvino
– as though Anto had not been mocking her father the night before –

her father had been so charmed he seemed to forget about his precious novel, had treated this stranger like a son; gripped his hand,

which Sophia remembered
pushing down on her head,
which Sophia remembered
wiping lipstick off her face,

her father had gripped it, and said, *what an impressive young man you are*

but not, Anto turned, as impressive as your daughter:
we often discuss
her book when we're together)

164

And the carpaccio has been taken from them, as though
this were the worst that could happen, as though it were
punishment;
    their waiter, stern,
    bending over the table
    again
    imploring them for silence, but Sophia's mother
    is talking –
    not to him – rather, between cackles,
    she is telling her daughter
    about the shame she felt
    on realising, despite everything,
    each time her ex-husband gave her another pathetic
    gift, how nice it was
    to be shown
    love,
    or something like it,

While Sophia's father wishes someone would show him
  grace
  instead of laughing:
  they're not aware
  of how closely this new actress
  resembles his ex-wife,
  they're not aware
  that the more they laugh
  the more he imagines his underwear may already be wet,

(And worse than the lie being exposed, what happened
after Anto had given
   a mangled explanation of Sophia's father's book – *isn't
she brilliant?* he'd said,
   you should be very proud
   and Sophia's father, after a moment's consideration
   had laughed too,
   in a booming way
   had explained who the real writer in the family was,
   my dear boy, he'd said, I'm very sorry,
   I hope she seduced you with more than that, I hope it's not
   the only reason you liked her, you poor thing,
   what a number she's played on you, you poor thing,
   prompting Anto
   to laugh as well –
She didn't seduce me, he'd said, she's a very lovely little
girl but I wouldn't think to touch her;

   neither of them had looked at Sophia while
   they laughed, while she had tried
   to get a grip on her shame)

And the waiter is insisting that it is time to leave,
    he has motioned
    for another server to approach with a card machine,
with the bill
    Sophia's mother is beyond herself
    she is chortling at the two men on either side of her
    who are telling her how inappropriate her behaviour is
    she says, *I'd love more wine,*
    she says, *I'm sorry to have disturbed your precious rota*
    each sentence is a joke only
    she knows the punchline for:
    Sophia desperately wants her mother to behave
    she wants to tell her about Anto ten years after the fact, but
    aren't you your father's daughter, her mother tells her each
time Sophia pleads or reasons
    that she is laughing too loud; that she has had too much
wine already,
    that they should talk about something else, besides which
    other lunch guests are quite cross
    at having the ordinances of their day
    disturbed,

And you're so perfect, the lead actor beams
   his new companion is as pure
   and perfect
   as the halo of blonde around her face: she has been doing
everything he asks primly,
   without a word of complaint, she has been sitting at the
upright end of the table as though
   it had all four legs:
   he has been praising her for it, he says he could marry
her, she's so good,
   it's hard to believe
   she exists,
   he might love her –
   is she real?
   Sophia's father tries to watch them embrace –
   but the woman is removing his alter ego's hands from
her torso
   and this really might be the final straw,
   this pathetic offering of love
   getting spurned:
   is this all

Sophia thinks he deserves?

the auditorium's audience is too dim to understand that for
their entertainment, he's being hurt
   and the auditorium's lighting is too dim to properly
check whether his pants have been soiled—
   Sophia's father rises from his chair:
   he is in pain,
   it won't leave him,
   he thunders,
   She will kill me in this play.
   She will kill me in this play.
   She will kill me in this play.
   She will kill me in this play.

The play stops.

FOUR:
EXIT, PURSUED BY HIS DAUGHTER

Sophia sits in her father's chair after the play's matinee is done. Quarter past five. The production team has just finished telling her what had happened: her father's timing had been exact, and the sound, like a gun – it cut through everything, and then stopped. He'd left on his own. Things resumed fluidly enough, after. The final half-hour of the play went undisturbed.

She's unsure where her mother is. She'd all but skipped out of the restaurant while Sophia fumbled with the bill and card machine, murmuring apologies to anyone who cared to listen. Their conversation hadn't finished: it had stopped, with no resolution. Now her mother has gone, she is elsewhere, continuing to have fun with the rest of the day. Now, Sophia puts her nails on the velvet where her father's arms must have gone; she pushes her weight down on the seat to make it equal to his. She can't, of course. The house manager approaches to ask if she's all right. The marketing director tells her she need not be out of sorts. Their faces are half covered and she can't tell whether their mouths match their words. A stagehand asks whether she wants to stay long – she can, of course, but there is cleaning to be done. Everything has to be disinfected before the evening run.

Sophia stands in the wings and watches her father's chair being sprayed with chemical agents until all trace of him is gone.

And of course you are right in wondering how Sophia's father felt, too; what happened after he left the play – and, of course, he felt ashamed at ruining the end of his daughter's work, but it was still the salve of the afternoon when this happened for him – the sun still shed some mercy for him; and of course, after running to the toilet and collecting his jacket, he stopped for gelato around the corner of the theatre, asked whether they had almond and melon flavours; and of course, the answer was no, would sir be interested in pistachio? and of course, he accepted two scoops of that and dulce de leche; and of course, it was horrifically overpriced; he stood for an extra half-minute counting out change from all the pockets he had; and of course, the couple behind him paid without flinching, paid with their fingers pressed to the bottoms of their phones – there was the swift *tap* of one machine to another; and of course, they sounded utterly happy; and of course, they were not aware of the devastation and the wreckage in his soul; and of course, they thought he was a rude old man when he barged past them with his cone, with his inconsiderate march, his stride, the slither of pink tongue curling shavings of flavoured milk into his mouth; and of course, there was something of the petulant schoolboy about it all – the huff and stamp and dessert to cheer him up; and of course, he got teary again when he remembered his age; and of course, he wondered, not for the first time, whether it isn't just a parent's lot to have to forgive the hubris of their young; and of course, he had a tough time swallowing this notion down; and of course, Sophia started calling his phone; it was beyond him to answer her now; and of course, the gelato was too much, too sweet, too ornately piled on its wafer shaft to withstand the pace of his walk – the sun was too hot; and of course, it began to melt down his hand in treacly brooks, candy green mixing into smooth brown – it all mottled, the colour of shit; and of course, this was just another thing gone wrong with his day; and of course, there were no napkins to save the sleeve of his jacket; and of course, nowhere to dump the melting mess except the floor; and of course, it earned him more dirty looks he felt he did not deserve, but the stickiness of his sleeve was the thing, it was a mission, it took over his mind and gave him purpose, put a dam in his eyes for the time being; and of course, when he diverted further into Covent Garden, the Tesco there loomed like a chapel, he had to rub gelled alcohol into his palms; and of course, he had forgotten to wear a surgical face covering – he had lost it somewhere; he did his best to hide his nose in his shirt – felt like an idiot; and of course, the Tesco was four times the size of his house, it was impossible to find anything, he began wandering in circles, now looking for face masks, now for napkins, could not find either, circled back, tried to focus on locating one, failed, tried to focus on locating the other, failed, became agitated, saw, without recognition, the same aisles over again, rows of pre-cooked salmon and sea bass, rows of whole, pre-buttered, garlicky chickens, and dairy, and vegan yoghurts; and of course, he began muttering to himself, a low grumble of *far too big* and *who needs this much food, consumerism gone too far*; and of course, he was not without self-awareness, realised he was an old man with ice cream stains on his suit growling to no one; and of course, he saw the middle-aged mothers with their dyed blonde hair and their offspring on a day out, their brows furrowing from stress, saw the rainbows thanking the NHS, saw the difference between the reverential lowering of those women's eyes before the stripes of red and orange and yellow and green and blue and purple, and how they looked at him, an old man with a touch of mania about him; and of course, he thought, *I have been you, too*, then questioned how right that was; and of course, whenever Sophia stayed with him, he'd always done the shopping beforehand to prevent the wasting of any of their precious time; and of course, this whole thing was pointless – he was standing where the toilet paper was, holding it together until wet little washlets caught his eye; and of course, he was put in mind of the years he spent wiping similar ones between his daughter's fingers and toes; and of course, he was asked to *please place his item in the bagging area*, and he did; and of course, he was asked to *please place his item in the bagging area*, and he lifted the washlets up and dropped them back down; and of course, *someone is coming to help you*; it was a man in a blue polo shirt who waved a barcode in front of the checkout screen a few times without even looking at him (did that count as help?); and of course, he wondered what he would have to do to get some fucking compassion around the place – did everyone in Covent

Garden just want him dead and gone? and of course, the lint in his pocket climbed its way up the sugar on his hand and sleeve as he withdrew change; and of course, the fifty pence he inserted trembled, the two pounds trembled, the one-pound coin rattled down and the sound of a penny dispensed sounded like bones cracking all over; and of course, by the time he came out of the store and began to walk home, his breaths were delivered to everyone around in great ugly sobs.

Like the luckiest of millennials beset with a habit of over-thinking, Sophia has a therapist. At half past five, she is preparing herself to run through the events of the day. She is fiddling with her laptop. She is adjusting the machine's neck until it sits at an angle that will flatter her jaw; propping novels under its base. The laptop is not on her worktable, which is behind her, but instead on a high stool, with another, slightly shorter chair in front. In her temporary office, the usual debris has been cleared onto the sofa in front of her, cushions adorned with last weekend's empty cans of Diet Coke, plates slick with the remains of a pasta lunch. A discarded sports bra, brown envelopes. Sophia is arranging a vase of lilies behind the camera's lens so they will fall just right of her shoulder. Despite being assured that no mental health professional worth their salt would ever project moral or aesthetic judgement onto her or her troubles, she performs this routine weekly.

Beyond the room Sophia stands in is a narrow strip of corridor laid with bad red carpet and punctuated with decomposing wooden doors. Bad changing-room light hangs above. The dressing-room-turned-office she is using had been a courtesy in the play's rehearsal period, and for the first few days of its run. It was supposed to allow Sophia access to everyone involved in its production; it was supposed to be a place where she could revise stage directions and think over suggested changes to the set from the artistic director. The actors should have been to be able to find her there and engage her in meaningful conversation about their characters.

The room takes even the most experienced of the theatre's janitors and runners fifteen minutes to find.

On pointing this out, Sophia had been told it was not customary for playwrights to have dressing rooms or offices. There were perks to having a famous writer for a father. She'd had to resist the impulse to reply that her father would have considered an expensed champagne lunch at J. Sheekey a perk, not a poorly converted basement office. For the duration of the play's run, she has been using it for scheduled video calls with a woman called Marlene. She has been seeing Marlene for eleven months.

Even therapy inspires a wealth of guilt in Sophia. When the idea to try it had settled, she'd found herself unable to face the triage of nine-month waiting lists per the National Health Service. Grudgingly, she had asked her father to extend the parameters of his private healthcare, and to her surprise, he had done so with no questions asked. That she was going to use it, exclusively, to quibble over every word he'd ever said to her was something Sophia did her best to ignore.

On the purple-bannered website of a Harley Street clinic, she had read the profiles of thirty-one neutrally photographed faces. She had run through the provided list of problems they could potentially solve. They had been laid next to each therapist's photo in alphabetical order. Abortion, abuse, addiction, adoption, alcohol, anger issues, behavioural issues, bereavement, bipolar, boarding school syndrome, borderline personality disorder, bullying, cancer, chronic fatigue, depersonalisation, depression, derealisation, domestic violence, erectile dysfunction, families, fertility, gender identity, general health problems, postnatal depression, premarital counselling, suicide, marriage, menopause, OCD, PTSD, relationship issues, self-esteem, self-harm, sexual problems, stress management, substance abuse.

Sophia had read through this and supposed that her life could be worse. But she had liked Marlene's profile because it said her practice was enriched by her knowledge of philosophy, theology, literature, and poetry.

How are you? is the question Sophia determinedly asks at the beginning of each session. It has never been answered satisfactorily. Today, Marlene opts for *very well*, before turning the query on her. Sophia has googled this woman for months and knows no more of her than the clinic website provided. Marlene might be married, she might not. She might have children, she might not. In their time together, Sophia has seen her wear floral blouses, white shirts, neutral eyeshadow. Marlene has well-cared-for hair, graceful hands, and a habit of drawing breath in unexpected places between sentences.

Your father saw your play today, she prompts. We have half an hour to speak now, and then you're due to see him, yes?

Maybe. I don't know. He's not returning my calls. Sophia explains the play's abrupt interruption.

Your father doesn't die in the play you wrote, is that right? Marlene says. Do you know what he could have meant by that?

183

It's not him, Sophia says. And no, on both counts.

Marlene is making notes, watching her with studied compassion. Her upper arm moves abstractly, guided by a pen and notebook Sophia knows is offscreen.

What do you write about when we talk? she asks. Marlene shakes her head once.

Okay, Sophia says. Truthfully, I don't understand him. Occasionally while I was writing this play, I looked for photos of him from when he was young. I don't have those kinds of memories of him. A lot of them are the same – he's usually at a party talking to women, or at his writing desk, or posed with some other nineties male friend, and there's always a cigarette in his mouth, and something between a sneer and a smirk. For some reason they're all in black and white. I don't think you could recreate those photos even if you found his exact double of thirty years ago and posed them against a perfectly replicated set. In all of those photos, he looks like he's having a kind of fun he'd be admonished for these days. I don't think I've ever had anything like that. He looks so unburdened. Life looks like it came so easily to him.

It's impossible to make assumptions about your father's mental state at any given moment, Marlene corrects her gently. You worry that he's unaware of the difficulties you encounter within yourself. It's possible you extend that very error of thought towards him.

All anyone does is consider his feelings, Sophia contends. I've been talking to you about him for months. I just had lunch with my mother and all she did was talk about him, too.

Tell me what she said.

Now Sophia shakes her head. It's not what she wants to discuss. Marlene makes another note.

184

The original draft of my play was a blow-by-blow account of the summer I spent with my father, Sophia continues. It was like a witness statement. But I was terrified of how he might respond. I revised an entire play for months in consideration of his response. And because it would have made me vulnerable in the aftermath. There would have been no way to talk about why I wrote it; its entire significance would have been lost to whatever corrections of fact he felt would be his due. All we have to work on between us is memory. I keep telling you how good he is at passing over what he doesn't like. He's a novelist. He's capricious.

So it is him, Marlene says. The main character. The play is about your relationship.

Sophia's finger hovers above the tab to end the call. She is in distress, and her therapist is playing *gotcha*.

Not very many women my age, Sophia exhales, get rewarded for writing about sex and parties in a straightforwardly comedic plot. It did occur to me that I'd be one summer's worth of entertainment at best and frivolous rubbish at worst. This play won't be received with the seriousness my father's work was. That's a luxury I have, she adds. To sit here, saying this. I don't mean it as a complaint. It's just something I wonder about. Her therapist watches her rearrange her features; sees the steadying breath in, which relaxes her mouth into a neutral position. I'm frustrated, Sophia says, by having come up in an age where bonding over trauma seems more correct than bonding over a shared laugh.

And in this case, Marlene says carefully, you've constructed an arrangement where an audience can laugh with you about your father.

185

Yes. Sophia blinks and looks at herself on call. The basement office. The sofa, and its pile of rubbish. The screen and its reflection of grey-looking lilies; the lilies themselves behind her, funeral white. I'm setting you a task, Marlene says, gaze directed offscreen, towards her notes. It's six o'clock. Go for a walk. Clear your mind. When that's done, call your father. If he doesn't respond, text him and arrange a time to meet so that you can discuss, clearly and directly, the play you wrote. We can carry the missing half-hour of this session forward to the next one. When she has finished speaking, the notebook comes into view, raised in a V against her open palm like a child's crude image of a bird. Before the call ends, she snaps it shut.

Sophia's father thinks he will write a *Garden of Earthly Delights*-like novel about the ridiculousness of contemporary life. He is aware that being an old man who used to overindulge in the joys of contemporaneity until it no longer suited him means that moralising or railing against them will make him look sour. He is aware that Bosch is a used reference point. But he is also convinced there is a way to make this work, and the mess of the Bosch, the joy of the Bosch, the hell of the Bosch strikes true for a reason. There is nothing wrong with the classics. He paces Covent Garden and works it out. His temples are strained from the effort of crying, and it's been ten years since he wrote a book. But it comes so quickly. Quickly, he realises that there is no nous to the reactionary novel – that even if he means it to be like fine art, this is how people write in their commercial novels, in their self-help books, in their Facebook posts and their tweets.

Therefore, he concludes, it's up to him to skewer it all. He has seen that so-called internet novels are on the rise. He thinks he could do a better job than most. He plans it: told like a parable, told like the Bible – the book could have an Old Testament and a New Testament. The book would describe wires and cables like branches and vine plants in some sort of Garden of Eden. Adam and Eve with Instagram accounts, photographing fruit. Mark, Matthew, Luke and John tweeting the gospels; Jesus, preaching via video conference. And then the masses, in their hordes, passing judgement on scripture: liking whichever of the commandments they find true and deliberating furiously in the comments on those they do not. He takes out his phone; makes slow work of googling the phrases he needs while sentences construct themselves in his mind. *Obviously thou shalt not kill, but not everyone has the socio-economic ability not to steal given the current minimum wage. Happy to keep the Sabbath but maybe a bit heteronormative to assume I would covet your wife?* He chuckles to himself. It would need some grounding mortal figure. He pictures a young woman, whose narcissism would stop the book from veering into proselytisation through the sheer absurdity of her character; one whose spoilt world view would narrow and warp the story of creation to a personal grievance turned social campaign. A woman so anally attuned to whether the world fits into her own version of morality or not that even the apocalypse cannot happen, since whatever revelation of knowledge it entails must first be clerically, painfully processed on her terms. In the end, the world would be ruined by her, not through divine revelations and dramatic falls of man, but through slow nit picking and equivocation until everything lost meaning. That would be the culmination of this new book.

Sophia has been calling. He's had his phone silenced since the matinee started at two o'clock, but it buzzes in his shirt pocket now, insistently against his heart.

It all feels like a joke. He comes back to the theatre's glass front. Good weather pours through it. The crowds inside drink it in happily. None of the young people he saw on his way into Sophia's play are milling there now. They were a trick of the light, for all he knows – everyone there looks his age, or only slightly below it: they are going about their day, examining programmes, talking to each other. He is the only person for whom the world is ending in carnage. He walks down to the Strand.

A little way down, standing outside the Savoy hotel, his ex-wife is gazing at its palm trees, wearing sunglasses and a nice shade of pink on her lips.

Before he has fully made the decision to do so, he is standing next to her. I've watched the play, he says.

She turns around at the sound, clutches her handbag closer in the crook of her arm before she realises it's him and lets it sway back. Fucking Jesus, she breathes. The sunglasses are turned up at the upper edges. The sun is catching all the blonde hair around her face, thickly dappled with grey. She only left him yesterday, but the play has made the day feel like a decade. Seeing her now is a revelation. He thinks she looks like a movie star.

I was thinking of checking in. Apparently, there's a spa. I've had a hard day, she tells him.

I have, too, he offers weakly. He thinks they could talk about it. In particular, about their daughter. The glasses obscure whatever she thinks of this idea. But she doesn't protest when he gestures for them to move further inside the hotel's entrance, out of the way of pedestrian traffic and passing cars. I take it, he says after she makes no sign of initiating conversation, that you know the gist of what the play's about?

She does. She's read it, it turns out. He tries very carefully not to show that this is a betrayal. You could have given me some warning, he tries. Did you talk to Sophia about it? I know she confides in you more than me.

Well, that's because I raised her, his ex-wife says pleasantly.

Sophia's father changes his mind. She doesn't look like a movie star. She looks like his ex-wife. The child support didn't hurt with that, he says and then, before she can answer, pivots away from the topic at once. I've been thinking, he muses, about how different the context of her twenties seems from mine. Less carefree. Girls like Sophia wake up to a torrent of difficulties in the world, some of which are pertinent to them, but often, ones they take on as voluntary burdens. They check their phones and feel obliged to shoulder a new social cause each week for fear of being deemed a bad person by their peers. But I hardly see a cause that isn't open to great swathes of criticism. How is it possible to achieve the already difficult goal of being constantly virtuous in an environment determined to see the bad in everything as a means to progress? I met a woman during the interlude of her play who was exactly this type of person – she seemed unwilling to admit the positive aspects of contemporary feminism and their benefit in her life. Being a good person, to her, involved an odd number of attributes I would use to deem a person dubious at best: a total unwillingness to be satisfied, a cruel instinct to lacerate, an ironic sense of snobbishness towards snobbery, a continuous condescension extended towards her peers for not being sufficiently aware of social injustice. In fact, she seemed to enjoy the idea of people she claimed to care about in distress. Their pain seemed to feed her ability to proselytise. Of course I wonder, what she would have to feel good about if they didn't exist?

I thought you wanted to talk about Sophia, his ex-wife says.

He does. He *is* talking about Sophia,

sort of. She looks unconvinced. What are you doing here anyway? he asks her. Are you going up for the evening run?

As a matter of fact, she sighs, I was having lunch with your daughter.

Your daughter is how he knows it didn't go well. When she is happy with Sophia, it is *my* daughter. When Sophia has done something she doesn't like, ownership is reverted to him. Now it is his turn to be pleasant. He starts to roll a cigarette. Before he licks the paper to seal it shut, he says, Did you have a nice time?

Did I, fuck. Sophia's mother examines the lustrous exterior of a Mercedes parked next to them. We've both been tortured, he tells her. The mention of lunch registers in his stomach. He asks her whether she'd like to try the hotel's restaurant. Don't, his ex-wife says. I'm not hungry. I don't want to eat with you anymore. I've had enough. I wanted to come here alone. If you want to have something, have it away from me. The past three months were enough.

It is important for her, he knows, to tend to his wrongs. Often, he lets her. It helps her feel better. She hangs them like wet laundry on his bones. When they dry, she takes them down and replaces them with others. It is never very long before she has cycled through to the original load. He enjoys the short intervals in which he can speak to her unburdened, when she pauses involuntarily with whatever sheet of grievances it is so important for her to hold and loses focus to laugh at a joke, to tuck hair behind her ears, to yawn. It was like this when they were married. She was pale, and fresh faced, and liked to take upon herself all kinds of harm. But at night, for a few hours at least, she climbed willingly into his arms. For this reason, he tries not to mind very much. For her, in this moment, he can pretend he's not hungry. He watches people go in and out of the hotel. He ignores the phone vibrating in his shirt's pocket.

Do you think, he asks when he has given her an appropriate length of silence, we've been good parents?

The problem with Sophia's mother is that she always knows exactly how to put his tail between his legs for him without ever raising her voice. All she says is, I've been a good mother to our daughter – and there's a magnanimity in that, which he knows he will never be able to achieve. It's one short, simple sentence that is impossible for him to replicate, even though he wants to have been good, too. She knows what she's done and takes pity on him. She pats his arm. Don't fuss too much, she tells him. It's not you.

He's aware there's a word the younger generation uses for what she's doing to him.

You're gaslighting me, he smiles. He conveys the mock indignation satisfactorily enough.

Oh, my dear, she says. Her hand is still on his arm. I'm not gaslighting you. I'm *lying*.

If he laughs now, he's sure the crying will not be far off. Nothing comes. He feels his ex-wife's touch rusting near his elbow. He has ruined the punchline of her joke; he has mishandled a moment of levity. Confirmation of her displeasure blooms across her face when he looks up: the sunglasses have come off; she is biting her lip at the entrance of the Savoy. It's a bit overpriced, he says to change the topic of conversation. She'd be better off finding a proper spa.

Wrong move. Somehow, in ways only she is capable of, he knows she has translated the assault on the hotel into an assault on her person. We need a good long break from one another, she informs him. I should have left your place months ago. You were insufferable.

He sighs. Who wasn't out of sorts? Those months had been life confined to video on demand, to a bed, to a sofa. There were days, he says, in which I was so bored.

We're in a pandemic, Sophia's mother says. People are dying. Service workers were risking their lives while you re-read *War and Peace* and stared at your indoor ferns. You're a terrible man, she tells him.

All the same. I missed our daughter, her ex-husband replies quietly. I wondered sometimes whether we should have asked her to stay. I wish we had. I had an image in my mind of you cooking dinner, the three of us laughing at the table, drinking wine—

Of *me* cooking dinner?

Sophia's mother shakes her head.

What are you going to do now? she asks. I don't want you crying at me down the phone again because the world isn't going the way you want. Explain to me how you intend to sort it out. She said the two of you were going to have dinner after the play. Has she called you?

She has.

Have you answered?

I haven't.

Of course. It's not as though you didn't spend all of lockdown whingeing that she never phoned you unless you asked her to.

Sophia's father is incredulous. I'm in shock, he says. I'm trying to work out how to salvage the situation. You have to help me. What's wrong with you? You seem ruffled.

You ruffle me, his ex-wife says, despite the fact that her voice has retained its way of remaining level at all times. It goes round his head like a Tannoy, low and penetratingly even. You're old enough not to blurt out every first thought that comes into your head. I won't tell you what I think of the play, and I won't get involved in your disagreement with Sophia. I'm tired, frankly, of debating with you. If you think what she's done is wrong, talk to her. Don't hang about gathering troops for your corner.

He leans back against the hotel's marbled walls. Ahead, tourists in matching hats stop to take photos of everything around them. In moments like these, where she treats him like a toddler, he likes to remind his ex-wife that she is not the only adult present. At last, he lights his cigarette. He tells her that he is planning to write a new book. The plot he came up with still sings in his mind. His ex-wife subjects herself to it, perched primly on one of the robust pots the hotel keeps its shrubs in. She thinks about how nice it would be to return home and find someone waiting there, ready to clean it from top to bottom, to take over her role as mother and ex-wife, to leave her free and unburdened. They would tell her that her work was over, that it was time to put her feet up.

Let me get this straight, she murmurs quietly once her ex-husband has finished outlining his novel to her. Ten years ago, you upset your daughter by writing a book she didn't like. Ten years later she has upset you by writing a play you don't like. And your solution to all of this now is to write another book. Yes?

Well, when you put it like that— Sophia's father starts to complain. But his ex-wife breathes, *Fucking artists*. She rubs her bottom lip unconsciously until her lipstick smudges. She leaves him on his own.

To a great show, the backstage crew for Sophia's play toast, and raise glasses of cordial in anticipation of the evening performance. They have been putting the stage back together again; they have been reconstructing the kitchen. In half an hour, a new audience will appear. You watch the set reacquire its form. A chair leg, previously shortened, is levelled back up. The table recovers its leg. Tiles are adhered back onto the walls with sheets of double-sided tape; it's a neat trick to get them, quickly, on and off. In the pockets of some of the staff are floor plans, which detail the progressive dishevelment of everything around them: they are working through them now in reverse. Time loops itself around the auditorium. Wilted herbs on the kitchen table are exchanged for fresh ones. Dust is swept off the floor. The willingness of red velvet chairs to hold unfamiliar bodies is born again, and in the theatre's glass extension, a new cohort gathers round. They are masked and clutching tickets, some paper, some digitised, with seat numbers printed in block capitals. They drink brandy, half-pints of beer, glasses of marked-up white wine.

In the tech booth, sound and cameramen are conferring. They are preparing to reshoot their previous effort in order to provide an on-demand streaming version of Sophia's work. They are checking the lights onstage. They are checking the sound. They are drawing up contingency plans in case it all goes wrong again.

Waterloo Bridge throbs with the city's unleashed footfall. Passengers ferry themselves across it with abandon. Past Covent Garden, past the Strand, wind blows lightly and freely over from one thin, flat side of its walkway to the other. The Thames below is a great grey bath, waving sluggishly up at Londoners in the heat of the summer.

Half heeding her therapist's advice, Sophia has chosen to walk back and forth along the bridge, thumb attendant to her phone. Now it hovers above the blue icon of a handset, now it flicks the contact page for her father up away from view. The next app open over to the left is Instagram. Sophia slows, lowers her neck, looks at a picture of a model she follows. Posted is a photo of her nude, stomach swollen eight months into pregnancy. Celebrities post the word 'Hot Mama' with heart-eye emojis and stars. Sophia calls her father. There is no response. Sophia calls her father. She worries there will never be a response.

Camphor and tweedy fabric collide with Sophia's nose. A man is saying, Fuck; a man is backing away from her, shaking his head with his collar upturned. Somehow, he is not sweating from the fever in the air. On his head is a flat cap, which looks old but not unfashionable. A version of his tapered trousers has been shown in *Vogue*, retailing at £3,000. Sophia's arm reaches out on instinct and he recoils; asks, Do any of you look where you're going anymore?

He seems the same age as her father. She moves away.

Sophia says, I'm so sorry, with the emphasis on the 'so', yet somehow this makes her seem insincere. The fug of the word, made longer than needs be, coils itself around his face and sours. You fucking kids, he says, which is rude enough on its own, might deserve rebuke, but what Sophia really wants to say is that she's almost thirty. Doesn't she look almost thirty? Isn't it clear that she has spent the day repressing enough desperation and anxiety for a person twice her age? She doesn't get a chance. He is pointing at her. Who do you think you are, walking around, looking at your phone? Are you aware of what's going on? You're not allowed to bump into people whenever you like. You're not even wearing a mask.

This is true and kills whatever argument she had been preparing. Perhaps, she thinks, he has been having a bad day also; perhaps this stranger is as wretched as her. She says, I'm sorry, again, but it doesn't work. What's so important on your phone? he asks. I want to know. You've risked my life. It must have been something important for you not to have been looking where you were going.

Her mouth opens and closes. It is late afternoon. It is hot, and there is a man, taller than her, shouting. He is demanding to see her phone. Sophia wonders whether she is safe – then recalls, this does not seem a plausible concern: he is intent on standing several paces away. Barriers of people continue to pass between them. The enforced distance emboldens her response.

I apologised. You have to stop. You can't just verbally abuse women in the street.

The disbelief in his face is so great, so comic, she wonders whether she's said something wrong.

Abuse? He laughs. I'm not abusing you.

You are, she says. Without her meaning to, her voice slips; starts to lack indignation. Ultimately, having you stand near me, swearing at me in a raised voice and demanding to invade my privacy by looking at my phone is incredibly frightening for me, and abusive of you.

The look he gives her brings her sharply back to where she is standing. The barrier of passing strangers has massed into a crowd. People have gathered to watch the street theatre operating on a pavement by the Thames. The man's voice, when it comes, is short, but it carries. You want to be careful, he says. What is it you do every day, with your nose in that phone? I'd like to know. What have you got on there that's more important than my life?

There is nothing she can think to say. He snorts, and continues on, away from her. Sophia looks round at the passers-by covering their mouths, avoiding her eyes.

Sophia's father has found a café on Long Acre to suit his mood. It belongs to a chain of others. On appraisal, he finds that both he and it are used up, worn out. After leaving his ex-wife, he had considered going home. He had thought about the steaks resting on the second shelf of his fridge, the drinks trolley in his living room. He could have made himself an early dinner. He could have had a drink. Put soap and water on the dishes when he was finished. Rubbed linen cloth on china. He'd imagined wiping the kitchen counter with a damp microfibre cloth the way he had seen his wife do it when she lived with him, and then gone upstairs to his bedroom and taken his socks off. Steam might have risen from the shower; palpitated above his head. The towel hanging on the rack nearby would have been crisp with detergent. By seven o'clock, he could have changed into a good pair of pyjamas and folded the sheets back on his bed. The desire to settle down; shift, until he found the perfect position on his back to rest in. The narcotic of having survived the day would have set in. He could have remained himself.

But Sophia kept calling. Now, he watches, from a chair

made up of cracked brown pleather, how immaculately the baristas scoop scones and nutmeg-flecked tarts from the display windows before them; the seriousness with which orders for drinks with milks he has never heard of are given. The hiss of steamers folds sinuously into the air alongside the burr of coffee being ground. Dolour.

Practicalities come to his rescue, incentivise him. To remain in the café, he will have to buy things. Yes, he will have to order himself a hot drink, with milk and brioche. And he will need the bathroom, to freshen up and feel better before the call. He eases himself out from the table.

The bathroom door is closed. A digital code lock protrudes from its top left.

The queue to the counter for coffee is long. When it is his turn to approach, the barista looks at him, bored. I'd like to use your toilets, Sophia's father says, and like clockwork the barista responds, toilets are for customer use only. Of course, Sophia's father assents. He could have guessed. But he needs the washroom before he orders; he is alone, with no one to guard his table. He will order something when he has finished attending to himself and is able to sit down properly.

His phone begins to vibrate again. Sweat pools under his arms. The barista is looking at him as though he's spoken another language, and a bad iteration of it at that. I can't allow you into the toilets unless you've bought something, sir, he says. It's protocol.

Uncharitable thoughts enter Sophia's father's head. The barista looks like a kid, doing time on a summer job. He has acne above his mask. His uniform is two sizes too big. He looks miserable, and he should be, enforcing meaningless dictums on people who might need a piss. Very probably, he still lives at the mercy of his parents, who place similar strictures upon him. Before the world collapsed, he likely went to school and endured, daily, the same insult in a different form. Sophia's father opens his mouth to complain again, to ask him where this man-child's backbone is, to put him in his place, and is stopped by the barista's silent gesture: he has lifted one finger to point at a horizontal sheet of A4 on which, in Times New Roman, is written, *Public Notice: We Will Not Tolerate Physical or Verbal Abuse Towards Our Staff.*

I'll have a coffee, Sophia's father murmurs. With hot milk. And brioche.

What kind of coffee? the barista asks.

A normal one.

But the barista has more questions. Would that be an Americano or filter? And what size? A normal size, Sophia's father huffs.

There's small, regular, and grande, the barista delivers in monotone. Please pick one.

The request elicits a hoarse laugh. Isn't normal a synonym for regular? Sophia's father asks.

It's not my place to make assumptions on behalf of the customer, sir. But may I point out that you're holding up the queue. Sophia's father turns around. He turns back.

A regular Americano, he grinds out. With hot milk on the side. And a brioche.

Eventually a black tray is placed in his hands. The code for the toilet, the barista notes in a drone well-accustomed to the difficulties of service work, is on the receipt. He sends Sophia's father on his way.

The tray is obnoxiously large. Coffee and milk slop out of their cups; mottle on its textured surface. And in the chair he had previously occupied, a woman is tucking into a packet of crisps. Fuck, Sophia's father breathes. There are no other seats. With care, he manoeuvres the tray towards the bathroom. He punches in the code to its door with one hand.

Getting his order into the toilet is a precarious act. He has to push the door open with his foot when it unlocks after he has managed to turn the handle without tipping the tray over; then turn, so that his back pushes the door further open, progressing into the bathroom with measured steps; then turn, so that the door is released, and he is facing the right way round. The door thuds shut.

For all the fuss it took to access, the toilet is the size of a coffin and smells like sour milk. A sanitary bin is overflowing with used pads and tampons. A clear spray bottle filled with blue liquid hangs desolately on the door's metal bar by its trigger.

There is no lid on the toilet seat. Sophia's father lowers the tray gingerly onto its cistern. It slips. He sets it onto the perimeter of the bowl, twists the lock on the door. In the bathroom mirror, the creased cotton of his shirt. The upturned lapel of his suit. Sophia's father washes his face, rinses his mouth with water. It is like starting the day over again – except he has no comb, and no amount of smoothing with his fingers will fix the lopsidedness of his hair. He wets it and regrets the decision instantly. Now the sweat-marked garments are accompanied by other darkened spots. He swipes hurriedly at the speckled canvas of his shoulders with wet hands until it resembles abstract art. There is nothing else to be done. He sees the hand dryer on the wall, hangs his jacket by the door and starts to unbutton his shirt, but Sophia is texting him insistently now; the phone rattles in the loosened fabric in short, staccato bursts. He pulls it out. She is asking whether they are still on for dinner.

The brioche bun sags pathetically on its plate, suspended by the toilet. He buttons his shirt back up. *Will call in a moment*, he texts back, and examines the damage he has done. Water clings to the fabric of his clothes. He can feel a pimple near his temple, a pointed, pressured dome. With little else to do, he picks up his coffee. He pours cooled milk onto its black. It's a small kind of comfort, holding the flooded mug. Carefully, once he has drunk half of its contents, he sits on the toilet and sets the tray on his knees. He takes the brioche out of its casing. He peels back each ridged triangle of paper and bites down.

I liked your play, he practises saying with his mouth full. Your play was good. I was watching the audience. The audience enjoyed your work. The audience liked your play. They thought it was good. You're a good writer. They think so. I think so.

Thick pulps of butter and flour stick to the roof of his mouth, his tongue. There is not enough brioche in the world to put off the next buzz of his phone, to balance its weight in one hand against the empty casing in the other. *When?* Sophia asks. *Now*, he replies.

Now. He lowers the tray onto the floor. It touches the tips of his polished black shoes. He presses down on the image of a video camera next to his daughter's contact details. When he releases it, he sees his image projected to him in miniature.

It looks like he's in a bomb shelter. Around him, greying green walls. Yellow light, which sinks into the lines under his eyes, magnifies the wet patches on his clothes. When his daughter's face supplants his, her cheeks drop.

He doesn't mean it to happen, but the first sound he lets out is a whimper. Too much smoking, too much bread stuck in his throat. Too much red around his eyes; they are swollen. Cherub, he tries again, and coughs.

Could we meet? Sophia asks. She sounds no steadier than he does.

I don't know, cherub, he hesitates. I'm very tired. I don't know.

But I've been trying to call you, she says. He nods. He knows the feeling, he tells her. Too often, he does. I can't always be the one who calls, Sophia's father coaxes. His voice becomes more desperate than he intends. Think of lockdown. It was always me reaching out to you. On that video chat business I barely knew how to operate. You have to call me, Sophia. You have to.

Shame on the screen, in the little pixelated box. She nods.

Is there a reason you don't? Is it . . . *ah*—

He can't help it, his eyes close—

. . . is it because of what you wrote in your play? Do you not like speaking with me anymore? Am I a bad person?

It's the first time he's asked the question of anyone.

I like speaking to you, Sophia offers quietly. I'd like us to talk now. Where are you? Could you come back to the theatre?

Her surroundings are so much more dignified than his. Behind his eyelids he can see the white lilies over her shoulder. He can see her mother's blonde hair cresting her collarbone. But there is something about the bathroom, the way it contains things. The way it makes them more manageable. What do you do when your play is showing? he asks. Do you watch it?

For some reason she has been waiting a few seconds after he has spoken before she responds. Sometimes, she says at last. Technically they don't need me there anymore.

His eyes open. Sophia is gazing earnestly at him. She goes on. Before press night I was in the wings in case any adjustments needed to be made to the lines or the stage direction. After press night, when everything was worked out, we made a schedule of one night a week for me to come. Mostly it just goes on. Without me. You know.

A whole new beast, he murmurs. Like with books.

Sophia nods.

The first apology is hers.

I'm sorry for not calling enough, she says. He accepts this with grace; manages to correct the front line of his hair.

All fine, he says. All fine. You're a busy young woman. Just something to be mindful of. I like to know how you are.

Silence transmits itself between their phones. The tip of his shoe nudges the tray forward.

The red carpet under Sophia's shoes is the speckled colour of a tongue. Periodically, she breaks her gaze from the shades of bile her father is wrapped in on her phone and looks to it for relief. For the duration of the call, everything her father has said has come fractionally after it's left his mouth. He is somewhere with poor signal.

Is there internet wherever you are? she asks him. Could you connect to it?

I don't want to, he sighs.

It would help the call, Sophia points out. It's taking forever to hear what you're saying on this end. Please? I'll guide you through it if you're not sure how.

The second apology is his.

I'm sorry, he says. I don't want to.

The past rolls in and shepherds with it all its wrongs. Sophia's face is a reprimand, emanating from his phone. She is unhappy with the quality of the call, and though she tries hard to smile benevolently at him, annoyance still shows through the cracks. Okay, he says. No point dancing around it. You've Me Too'd me. Is there anything I'm allowed to say? Or will it end up in the sequel?

Annoyance wins out. Now his daughter is scowling rather than caring, on the turn of a second. Obviously you can say things, Sophia snaps. Objectively appropriate things. Anything that doesn't insult the dignity of the people around you.

She sounds like her mother. It makes him want to cry all over again. It's a good play, he attempts, I saw the audience enjoying it. Only the words come out wrong; they are so short, and so dull, and so unlike the way he had practised. She shakes her head at him as though she is disappointed.

Was it me? he asks finally.

He thought he'd softened his tone. He thought he'd delivered this question kindly, without accusation, but to his horror, Sophia's face puckers on the screen. It's not clear why. The sound of snot and snivels sit haplessly in his palm. Even over the phone, with poor connection, he can tell that, at twenty-eight, his daughter cries exactly the way she used to as a child.

Yes, she says. It was.

He's never seen another person who cries the way she does. He can't think where she learnt it from. When she was little, and something was wrong, she would go mute for hours at a time with tears rolling down her face until whatever was troubling her went away. He used to watch her mother reprimand her for ten, twenty, thirty minutes at a time over some silly thing while Sophia stood in silence, biting her top lip. Then, after she'd been sent to her room and a few minutes had passed, he'd go up to put a reassuring hand on her back as rivers came out of her eyes.

It's hard. He doesn't like to see her cry; would do any-thing to stop it – but hadn't he unravelled in the very same way only an hour ago because of her? Shouldn't it be her comforting him?

Why? he pleads finally.

She doesn't answer. He watches her sob through a phone.

Sophia, her father is coaxing her over video call. Sophia, come on. Please answer.

She can't. She hasn't had time; hasn't managed to prepare counter-arguments for his questions. She is angry, but the feeling won't come coherently, the way it does for others. It comes as tears.

This is so pathetic, she hiccups while mascara comes down her chin – but her father doesn't understand that she is referring to herself. Now he models anger for her. She wishes she could carry it off half as well as him. He begins to bark questions down the line. They come so effortlessly from his mouth, increasing in volume and vigour each time. What is the play supposed to mean? Could she not have warned him about it? Was it really necessary to have put it on at all? Did she not think of how upsetting it would be for him to watch her distort his character and his work?

Sophia thinks that if she could just adopt the same tone of voice,

If she could interrupt the barrage of questions emanating from her phone,

Or if he would speak to her calmly, without shouting, and let her gather her thoughts—

But that's why I didn't tell you about the play, she tries. I didn't want to be overly influenced by you, because you can be so incredibly heavy-handed without seeming to realise it. It's not just me; Mum thinks so, too. I'm obviously very sorry about any discomfort you feel but it's the same discomfort you place on everyone around you. And now you won't even pause long enough to let me speak.

No, no, he interrupts. Let's not skirt around the facts. You've misrepresented me, you've misrepresented my novel—

Sophia wishes she could shout without hearing her voice tremble.

Fuck your novel, she gasps. I hate your novel. It made me feel exactly the same way Elena's nephew did.

She closes her eyes and begins to tell her father about Anto.

His nose has not acclimatised to the stench in the toilet. Each time he moves, new notes are added to it. Fish and disinfectant. Sophia's protests are spilling ardently out of his phone, presenting images he does not care for, many of which are repetitive in nature. A boy's fingers against his daughter's mouth; another tongue on his daughter's tongue; an arm tightened around her torso; a hand pushing her head down.

Enough, Sophia's father says. The handle on the bathroom door makes an inquisitive turn. He stands up and puts his back against it to wedge it shut. I don't need details, he says.

That's fine, she snaps. That's not the issue anyway. You had me write that shitty book, and then instead of talking to me about it, or spending time with me, you made me listen to you having sex with different women every night – did it ever occur to you to at least *try* acting like a parent?

It is impossible to keep up with the speed of her accusations, quietly cultivated over years. That she expects him to come up with a response in mere seconds seems grossly unfair. He takes stock of his sins. He didn't spend enough time with her; he unwittingly sent her on a few bad dates. He was insufficiently paternal – though he disputes this last claim. He's sorry, he says. Is that what she was after? Could they not have resolved this earlier? Could they not have saved themselves the bother of her play ruining his novel and his good name?

The important thing seems not to cry, himself. He wants her to know that what he's saying is rational. He finds a spot just above his phone's camera and talks to it.

And what of her sins? In this entire conversation, has she bothered to ask how he is? She has served him the worst day of his life on a shitty paper plate, and *somehow*, there he is, apologising in response. Does that seem right to you, Sophia? he asks. Or is there something I've misjudged?

You don't think you could have done better? his daughter asks, as though it's a question he doesn't walk round his head multiple times a month. If only his ex-wife could see them now.

No, he says stoutly. The bathroom door has started to rattle, its handle pressed down.

Somewhere along the way, she's developed a blocked nose. It makes her sound extremely young.

You don't think it was unnecessary to spend the only real quality time we've had in our lives fucking random strangers?

Get over yourself, he barks. Evidently you were doing the same elsewhere.

Sophia's face freezes soundlessly for so long he wonders whether there's something wrong with his phone.

That's the worst thing you've ever said to me.

Her voice comes softly into the bathroom's dirty green walls. Millimetre by millimetre, the door to the bathroom

214

rocks back and forth, gathers speed, until his body, the mirror on the wall, the dispenser with paper towels, the pull cord for the bathroom's light are all set in equal motion. Panic sets in. You know, I'm sorry it didn't work out with your mum, he says hurriedly while everything quivers. I'm sorry I didn't take on more of the childcare; I know she was better than me at that. I'm sorry we didn't go on a normal holiday. I'm sorry I let you go off with that stupid boy.

By now, the barista's drawling monotone has started coming through the crack between the door and the ground below, asking Sophia's father whether he is in need of medical assistance.

You're in the theatre, he tells Sophia; gathers his jacket. I'm going to come to the theatre. His trousers come away damply from the toilet's bowl as he rises, adhere themselves to the sweat around his thighs. Don't move, he says. We're not done. We're going to fix it. Just wait for me by the entrance.

She has been looking at him unsmilingly without hanging up. She gives no indication of whether she will wait for him or not. It is unclear whether, if he ends the call, she will feel absolved of the need to look at him anymore. I'm going to hang up, he decides aloud. But I'll be with you in ten minutes. Five. I'm around the corner.

Getting out of the café is an ordeal on its own – there is the barista, tiredly pacifying an upset customer; there is the customer, insisting that it is the shop's legal obligation to provide a bathroom. Blocking the door also is another member of staff, who takes Sophia's father by the shoulders and tries to guide him to a chair. They offer water, they ask in hushed tones whether he feels short of breath, or fatigued, or congested, or nauseous. Sophia's father does his best to contain his irritation, and gratitude, and anger, and dread.

On freeing himself from them, he rushes back to the theatre. Seven o'clock. He searches its glass entrance. No sign of her. He walks each flight of stairs through the building, describing her to strangers in case they've seen her. I'm looking for my daughter, he says. She's blonde, brown eyes, wearing a blue top.

How old is your daughter? one elderly woman asks. Would you like me to notify a member of staff that she's missing?

There is not enough time to explain. But the misunderstanding prompts another thought. Although he can't

216

remember the name of the woman who showed him into the tech booth, he asks after her at the front of house, identifying her by her role and the colour of her hair. She is discerned and discovered. He asks whether his daughter is still about, and she says yes. He asks whether there is a room he could sit in, whether it is possible for her to be brought to him as soon as possible. He can see that the head of brand engagement and social media finds it a nuisance, but also that she is not entirely sure whether it's a request Sophia might have preferred enacted or not. All the same, she hurries him into an elevator, takes him through the corridor he has walked once already. They go past the ramp that leads to the auditorium, and she glances back at him every so often with a forefinger pressed to her lips.

She takes him backstage. From there he sees that the whole thing extends further back than most people watching from the front would imagine – that the stage visible from the red velvet seats in the auditorium itself comprises less than a third of the total space it takes up. He sees that there are more crew in black clothing than he had imagined earlier that afternoon, some with make-up brushes tucked into pinafores, some holding bottles of water and hoodies that plainly do not belong to them; some with headsets they murmur almost indistinguishably into. Around them, the sound of a woman orgasming. Sophia's play has begun its evening run.

The head of brand engagement and social media walks him to two large silver doors and presses a large silver button on them – waits, until they part. He notices that she has been eyeing him nervously for the duration of their walk. Now, at last, with the presence of others around him, he realises what was wrong, and hides the lower part of his face with his jacket while they descend. She does not relax.

When they come out of the lift: none of the grandeur of above. Low ceilings and a dirty brown floor; a few cardboard boxes stacked opposite them, and several doors. She takes him through one at the furthest end from where they have come: everything becomes a white room with exposed light-wood beams above them. It has a particular luminescence. Once his eyes adjust, Sophia's father sees that half of the room is cluttered with tables and benches, strewn with more wooden frames, more cardboard boxes, power tools. His guide gives him little time to take it in. Another door. Then sinews of fluorescent corridors and more railings, stacked up against each other so closely that they begin to resemble cages. He continues to follow her until, seemingly at random, she reaches out. Her hand pushes part of the tall white walls. It swings open. The process looks like magic to him: she knows where to put her palms so that new places can appear.

It has all been here, he thinks, this whole time, in a series of colourless, LED-illuminated halls. Every so often, the woman pushes open parts of white wall and lists people and their jobs as and when those people pass: wigs work-room manager, props assistant, director of audiences and media, head of operations. We've started to keep those more corporate offices in-house, she says. They used to be in a separate building about twenty minutes' walk away. That was another change made along with the renovated front of house. It's good. It makes our content online more authentic. I think people are getting savvier now. Theatres don't just run on costume departments and nice sets.

Of course, of course, Sophia's father murmurs distract-edly. Everything's a business now.

Very true, she tells him, and pushes another wall. This time, carpet meets his feet. If you don't mind just waiting here, she says to him. It's a dressing room, but no one's using it at the moment. I have to ask you not to leave unless it's an emergency. There's a toilet down the corridor – it's marked on a door to your right. There's water here – she taps a plastic bottle – and, uh, Wi-Fi password ... She digs into her back pocket for a notebook; transcribes randomised letters and numbers onto a scrap of paper. I'll give you my number as well, although again, I have to ask you only to use it for emergencies. I'll have your daughter meet you here shortly. More numbers on paper. She leaves them in his hand.

By the time Sophia has finished packing her bag in the aftermath of her call, the head of brand engagement and social media has contacted her. Her father, she is told, is in one of the basement's disused dressing rooms. He is surprisingly easy to find. When Sophia enters, he is standing near the furthermost wall from the door.

They face each other.

His heart is migrating to places all over his body; he feels its beat in his forehead, his ears, his wrists, his neck. She is solid, unmoving. Then, softly, they switch. He calms, steadies, while her shoulders lift up and down with short bursts of breath. They count sentences separately in their minds, together. Him: *I love you and I have become scared of you; I think you're wrong, but I'm sorry for now; let's forget it all.* And she: *I love you but I have stopped idolising you; I know you think I'm wrong, but I'm not.*

At last he says, I didn't tell you.

Sophia waits for him to continue.

He swallows. He looks at her reddened nose, the swollen skin around her eyes.

I didn't tell you, he repeats, that you're a very gifted writer.

You've constructed a good play. The audience liked it very much.

She inhales.

You did say that. But thanks for saying it again.

They look at each other. Thanks, Sophia repeats. Neither says anything else. Time moves between them, over them. They stand at opposite ends of the room. Neither moves, though each waits for the other to close the gap. For a moment, they bargain silently, wait to see who will be the one to cast a final verdict on the matter.

Sophia forces a smile. Shall we go to dinner? she asks. Her father looks at her. He takes off his jacket.

Before we do, he says, I really don't mean to argue, cherub, but I think it's worth just one last time us going over—

The head of brand engagement and social media's palm pushes the slab of wall closest to Sophia open, and the phone in her hand enters the dressing room before she does. I'm sorry to interrupt, she says brightly. Do excuse me, it won't take long. Only I thought we could get a photo of you two together. Talented daughter taking after proud father, you know. I thought you might want to preserve the memory. And if you're comfortable, maybe share it with our audiences? I'm sure it's exactly the sort of thing that would lift their spirits if they saw it. Full of love.

Sophia's father wants to protest and finds he can't. There is too much open sincerity shining out of her face; it's as though she believes in what she says. When both he and Sophia remain mute, she continues gently on. I think it's a good message to attach to the play, you know, men supporting women; one generation leading on into another. Not that I want to turn your relationship into a marketing stunt. Very much the opposite. I think a photo like this would resonate with a lot of people in an authentic way. What do you two think? Is that okay?

Neither Sophia nor her father answer. The head of brand engagement and social media beams. She takes Sophia's father gingerly by his elbow, the way nurses in films handle the infirm.

Great. If you could move closer to me and, Sophia, you go – move closer—

She steps back. The slight crescendo, the suction noise of an iPhone unlocking, resonates around them. Sophia and her father listen to the sound of nails hitting glass, watch her head momentarily drop, then lift in tandem with the screen when she raises the device to them.

Ready? she asks.

They draw closer. They put their arms around each other, his looped low across her back, hers reaching across the top of his shoulders. They smile until they register the sound of an imitation aperture: once, twice. Oh, wonderful, she tells them. You both look wonderful. Take a look.

She turns her phone to them and they detach, lean forward and examine the portrait. Sophia thinks, *I look tired*, and her father thinks, *I look old*. The head of brand engagement and social media pivots herself so that they can watch her thumb swipe until it finds the requisite blue icon with its block-white outline of a bird, watch it hover over, then tap an icon of a quill and a plus symbol. They watch her type, 'Like father like daughter', and attach the photo with its requisite hashtags. She sends the tweet. Finally, she looks up at them. You know, you look so alike close up, she says to Sophia's father. She's really got the shape of your mouth and nose. And there's something about the character of your faces, too. She looks back at her phone again. Oh wonderful, she exhales again. The sound is breathy, ecstatic. It's already getting likes. Thank you, she tells them, still looking at her screen, for sharing that with us.

Ten years ago, Elena had arrived at the house Sophia and her father had borrowed in Sicily on the morning they were due to leave. She had let herself into the house with her own set of keys, placed them on the table near the door. She'd checked her make-up in the mirror above it; wiped stray flecks of blue glitter from under her eyes and shook her fringe out until it arranged itself neatly over her brow. Then she'd turned to look down the stretch of corridor that attended the front door. She'd called out to announce that she had come.

Sophia's father had appeared; he had flung his arms towards her. He advanced with his walk of an old Englishman; she'd always noted this about him. She wondered whether all ageing people in England walked the way he did – neck bent, body angling towards the ground. It reminded her of a turtle. At first Elena had put this down to his lack of exercise. In all the time the two guests had spent in the house, she had only had to wash Sophia's swimming clothes. She had never seen him do more than look at the sea; do more than walk leisurely towards a shop or a bar. Slender as he was, he ate non-stop: he tore chunks of bread off loaves when passing through the kitchen, picked up nuts and fruit wherever he found them and deposited them into his mouth – he consumed constantly. Somehow, it showed. In fact, though they were likely the same age, while she moved around the house with a broom and a mop he often murmured, *Ah, Elena, you make me feel like an old man. Ah, Elena, you're a lightning bolt.* When he first said it, and she had not fully understood, he had mimicked the sound of thunder. *Electricity in a storm,* he said, *that's what you are. A proper glamour puss, with that electric make-up of yours. But you leave tidiness rather than chaos in your wake.* Then she became *Elena the lightning bolt.* It was what he said while he progressed towards her, still slow, still mannered.

We're scraping around the house, he said. *We seem to have lost everything we arrived with.* She asked him to list what was missing. *Oh, combs, shirts, pens and notebooks. Cables and chargers. Knick-knacks, silly things.* He did not seem concerned. *Better try not to litter someone else's house, but we won't spend much longer. If it's gone, it's gone,* he shrugged. *Would you mind making sure Sophia's packed?*

She did mind but said nothing. Sophia was in her room, at her laptop. Father and daughter had not been speaking very much for the past week, as far as Elena could tell. She seemed sullen. The clothes in her suitcase were unfolded. On most of the available surfaces the room had to provide were bottles of nail varnish and rinds of fruit, bikinis and T-shirts strewn over chairs and dangling out of the dresser, flip-flops patterning the floor. She was not ready to go.

Time to pack? Elena suggested from the door. The girl didn't move. In this, she was like her father. She turned and said, *we still have two hours before the boat.* Elena shook her head and began taking clothes out of Sophia's suitcase;

folded them back in lengthways, as flat as they would go. Sophia watched her, bored. Since Anto had come back from his last meeting with her, Sophia had fallen in Elena's estimation. Anto said she was cold, and rude. She was demanding in the worst way an English tourist could be. He said she had made no effort to learn Italian, so that she could speak with him to his friends. He said he had taken her to the best places he could think of in Vulcano, and she had merely taken pictures without looking; had not stopped to admire what was in front of her for more than the time it took to raise her phone to it. Sometimes she took pictures of herself next to flowers or volcanic rock, as though she were equal to how majestic they were. She had told him she was writing a book, only for it to turn out that it was her father's. *She has ideas about herself*, had been Anto's verdict. *You know, I understand: she is very young, a little immature, but still – too rude. I think she is very selfish. She thinks only of her own pleasure.* After he had said it, Elena realised it, too. What she had first taken for shyness became rudeness in contrast with Sophia's father's pleasant way of being. True, sometimes her father ingratiated himself a little too much, but he never left Elena alone while she cooked dinner for him and his daughter; he understood how to be social, how to speak out loud and keep company. The younger one often seemed as though she had many thoughts but never shared them, seemed always oblivious to decencies a person should show when they were not the only one in the room. Sophia sat over her laptop, or notebook, or phone, and ignored what went on around her. They had never had a proper conversation.

After a few minutes of Elena gathering rubbish into a wastebin, smoothing out creases in skirts before packing them into the suitcase, Sophia looked at her quietly and said, *You don't have to pack my things for me.* Yes, she was very rude. Even when she added, *Thank you, Elena. I'll do it myself now*, she did not use the right tone. Elena took the bin and closed the door behind her. Across the corridor, she found Sophia's father, his room as much a mess as his daughter's, though he seemed to fuss over gathering things into a pile: never accomplishing much beyond an increasing mound of detritus. She went into the room. She couldn't see his suitcase.

It's on top of the wardrobe, he said. *No, I'll get it, don't you worry.* He heaved it down; spread it open on the bed. When she began to pack his shirts for him, he sat down next to his luggage and, beaming, told her, *Elena, you're a saint. Grazie, grazie. I don't know what this excursion would have been without you.*

And you have finished the book? she asked him. *Almost, almost. A few month's hard work. It's been very tiring, you know. Not much of a holiday in a way. I'm sure I won't be surprised if it turns out that going home comes to be something of a break in itself. We've both been longing for our own beds now. But –* he corrected himself at once – *that is, of course, no slight on your incredibly generous hospitality. We should have thought of a gift to get you. Or invited you to dinner last night. What an oversight on our part. You won't think too badly of us?*

Elena smiled and brought the hem of his folded jeans up to their waistband; laid them in the case. You can give me a present, she said. You can make a dedication to me in your book. A grand gesture. She watched his conscience absolve in real time across his face: the dawning relief. *Excellent idea,* he laughed. *Right at the front. I'll do that.*

An hour and a half later, both suitcases were packed. She

accompanied them to the front door. They put on their trainers and Chinese hats sold in tourist shops; they shuffled about around her. *Sophia*, her father prompted. The girl cleared her throat. *Thank you so much, Elena*, she said, and allowed two civil kisses on either cheek. She raised her eyebrows at her father, opened the door and stood outside.

Compliments to the owner of the house, Sophia's father chuckled while he and Elena embraced. *What a lucky man, having two women like his wife and you to keep him. If I thought I could sway you to come back to England and live in with me, Elena, I would. In an instant. How much would I have to pay you?* She shook her finger at him in mock warning. *No, no, no, no. Of course, that would never do. What could a damp little island offer you that you don't have here in paradise?* He handed her his set of keys. *Arrivederci, bella Elena.* He kissed her four times on either cheek.

After they left, Elena put their keys beside her own on the side table and proceeded into the house once more. First the kitchen. She had cleaned twice a week and still it was a mess. Knives smeared with oil and butter formed nests with stained forks in the sink: plates patterned with egg yolk overlaid them. The fridge smelled of fish; they had left the seafood she'd brought them a week ago uncooked in a bottom drawer. Breadcrumbs on the table. A pot starched with pasta water still on the hob. The amenity of the kisses Sophia's father had placed on her cheeks began to wear off. She shook her head while she poured boiling water over the dishes in the sink and washed them; she shook her head while she scoured the tiles surrounding the hob. They had left too much food behind; she put as much as she could into a bag to take home and threw the rest away. She thought of the waste. When she swept the breadcrumbs off the table, then out the door with a broom, her back hurt: the muscles of it strained between her shoulder blades. She felt it each time she reached to replace the cups and pans to their cupboards; to their hooks affixed to the walls. And the smell Sophia and her father had left was unpleasant. It was bodily, it had undertones of sweat covered with powder and cologne – faint, but detectable nevertheless over the herbs she had continually brought in. Elena squeezed lemons into boiling water; opened the windows and rubbed the inside of the fridge and oven down, then the floor until the kitchen smelled clean again.

It took two hours. Then the bathroom, still wet with their morning's showers; the front room – used tissues tucked into the armrests of the sofa, stains on the carpet. Their rooms, and the time spent stripping bedsheets from each mattress to put them in the washing machine to launder. Sophia's father had been right. Their possessions remained; ruined the tidiness of the place long after they had gone. Bits of notepaper scribbled on, stray books, hairbands, pens, several earrings, none of them paired, empty bottles of water, plastic cutlery. It was all there. They were lazy, messy people, Elena decided. She had watched them for a month, idling around the house, declaiming things at each other, never bothering to make her job easier with the simplest of acts – wiping down sinks, or picking up after themselves. To think she had brought them freshly picked oranges each time she came. She carried a black bin bag from room to room, throwing everything of theirs she found into it. When she had finished cleaning, she took it with her to the front door and picked up both sets of keys. She looked at herself in the mirror once more. Sweat had caused her make-up to run. Blue eyeshadow pooled at the rims of her eyes, in their creases. Her hair stood up around her face. She examined the lines near her mouth, now more prominent, it seemed, with the effort of her labour, the cost of her displeasure. They had aged her, made her look like an unkempt old woman. Elena shut the door behind her and walked towards the beach with a bag full of their cast-offs. It went into one of the public bins. A year later, Sophia's father sent her a copy of the book he had written while she had cleaned around him and his daughter. Scrawled in pencil rather than ink on the title page was, *Grazie, bella Elena.*

She threw that away, too.

Acknowledgements

My thanks to:

Harriet Moore, Sophia Rahim, David Evans;

Ana Fletcher, Alice Borges, Thom Insley, Rosy Cooley;

Gaby Wood, Ben Okri;

Lettice Franklin, Naomi Gibbs, the teams at Weidenfeld and Pantheon;

and Charlie Hammerton (for, among other things, a good story about a fish tank).